EXPLAIN THIS . . .

A slab of metal, two meters square by several centimeters thick, appeared on the ground in front of him, shiny purple-black. Spock rose, trance-like, and picked it up with one hand.

He put both hands close together on an edge, then pushed with one and pulled with the other. The metal bent slightly, with a deafening high-pitched creak. Where it was bending, it glowed red-hot . . . then orange, then yellow, then white—the blinding white of a star's surface. The others had to look away, and shield their faces from the heat.

With an awful rending sound, the slab gave way; Spock ripped it all the way through and dropped the two pieces. They fell heavily to the ground and imbedded themselves to a depth of several centimeters.

"Very odd," Spock said. He started to touch one of the slabs but felt the heat radiating from it, and withdrew. "Tritanium is 21.4 times as hard as the best steel.

"The illusion I experienced was of tearing a sheet of flimsy paper."

PLANET OF JUDGMENT

Joe Haldeman

BANTAM BOOKS

TORONTO • NEW YORK • LONDON • SYDNEY • AUCKLAND

PLANET OF JUDGMENT
A Bantam Book / August 1977
4 printings through June 1984

Star Trek is a trademark of Paramount Pictures Corporation
Registered in the United States Patent and Trademark Office.
Published by Bantam Books under exclusive license with
Paramount Pictures Corporation

Copyright © 1977 by Paramount Pictures Corporation.
All rights reserved.
Cover art copyright © 1984 by Enric.
mimeograph or any other means, without permission.
For information address: Bantam Books, Inc.

ISBN 0-553-24168-0

Published simultaneously in the United States and Canada

PRINTED IN THE UNITED STATES OF AMERICA

H   13 12 11 10 9 8 7 6 5 4

"The universe is not only queerer than we imagine. It's queerer than we can imagine."

—SIR ARTHUR STANLEY EDDINGTON

1

The crew's morale seems high in spite of the four-week detour. This morning's maneuvers went well; this afternoon Mr. Scott has a drill planned. I think we have been successful in promoting the feeling that the Enterprise is on vacation—rather than having been forced, by vagaries of scheduling, into a mission that a transport or scout could accomplish as easily.

I haven't yet met our supercargo, Dr. Atheling, other than formally welcoming him aboard ship. Mr. Spock speaks highly of his reputation in astrophysics, and several of the crew know him from Academy days.

By tomorrow the maintenance and training schedule should be complete; I look forward to meeting a man important enough to shanghai a month out of a heavy cruiser's schedule.

Captain James T. Kirk leaned back in the soft command chair and appeared to be daydreaming. In fact, he was counting seconds.

Mr. Sulu was to take over the bridge for a shift beginning at 1200. It was 1159, and for the past couple of minutes Sulu had been casting anxious glances at

1

the captain, evidently wondering whether to interrupt his reverie.

At precisely twelve, and without looking toward the chronometer, Kirk stood. "Mr. Sulu?"

The helmsman was already on his feet. "Yes, sir."

"If you will take the bridge . . ." As Kirk passed Sulu on his way to the turbolift, his eye flickered in what might have been a wink.

At the messroom, Kirk punched up ham and eggs, double ham to compensate for missing breakfast, and sat down across from Dr. McCoy.

"Howdy, Jim," McCoy said over the rim of a coffee cup. "Long shift this morning?"

"Not too bad, Bones." More softly: "Does it show?"

"Only to a highly trained observer, such as myself. An acute student of the human race. Bags under your eyes."

Kirk applied himself to the ham and eggs. "I've sort of been on double duty," he said between mouthfuls, "without Mr. Spock. Didn't want to call him out of meditation, but setting up this busywork schedule has turned out to be more complicated than we'd expected."

"As usual," McCoy said. "If I were captain of this vessel, I'd give the crew four weeks off. Let them catch up on their reading, play some—"

"Good thing I'm captain." There was just a touch of hardness in Kirk's friendly voice. "Hate to see you presiding over the second mutiny in Star Fleet history."

"I know what the book says, Jim. I think the book underrates the maturity of the crew."

Kirk blew on his coffee. "You're probably right. But there's no harm done this way, and at least the ship'll be in perfect order when we put in at Academy."

"What difference does that make? We'll beam down the professor and move on."

"Maybe. Maybe not."

"Come on, Jim. What do you know that I don't?"

Kirk began carving up his second piece of ham. "I'll resist the obvious answer to that—"

"You're just afraid to hear what *I'd* say."

"Possibly. Do you know Commodore Martin Lawrence?"

"Haven't had the pleasure."

"No pleasure. He's chief of Starship Flight Training, at Academy. I once had some words with him."

"So?"

"So I suspect that, strictly as a learning experience for the cadets under his command—no reflection on my abilities as a commander, of course—he'll ask that the *Enterprise* be put through a Class I inspection."

"I think I see."

"Yes. Everything has to be correct, down to the last molecule. I suspect it will be a very careful inspection."

"What a crazy way to make a living."

They ate in silence for a minute. "What's that commotion over there?" Kirk asked. At a table across the room, two men were having a spirited argument. They were James Atheling, the professor they were carrying to Academy, to become the new dean of Star Fleet's College of Science, and Andre Charvat, a senior science officer who was second only to Mr. Spock. Another science officer, Sharon Follett, was also at the table, looking bemused.

"They arguing physics? I've never heard of this Chandler fellow."

"Neither have I, but it's not physics. I doubt

they'd wax so passionate over physics. It's a hobby they have in common."

They listened. "Ah, I see," Kirk said. "It's some kind of literature."

"If you want to call it that. Twentieth-century American detective fiction—from what they were saying before you came in, I take it that Charvat is defending an author named Hammett, and Atheling prefers a later writer, named Chandler."

Kirk shrugged. "The only one I've ever heard about is Sherk, uh, Sherlock Holmes . . . seems like a small thing to get so hot and bothered about." He shoveled the last of his eggs onto a piece of toast. "That's the way people are about their hobbies, I guess."

"In this case, I think it's more the way Charvat is about Atheling, and vice versa."

Kirk raised both eyebrows. A starship runs on gossip; even the captain isn't immune.

"I was talking to Follett," McCoy said quietly. "They all know each other through the Academy; know each other pretty well. Atheling was a young instructor when Charvat went through Academy, one of the best in any department. Charvat opted for teaching, too; taught for a couple of years, and then decided he'd rather have space duty."

"Don't blame him," Kirk said.

McCoy nodded. "He's done well. But it's undeniable that Atheling's done better, staying in academia."

"So what? That's comparing apples and oranges."

"True, unless you happen to be the apple. And Follett complicates things."

"Women always . . . in what way?"

"Well, now, this is only my own opinion."

"As 'an acute student of the human race'?"

4

"As a person with two eyes. Follett went through Academy ten or eleven years ago—"

"Graduated eleven years ago," Kirk said. "Second in a class of 286." Kirk knew his officers.

"Of course. Atheling was a full professor and department head by then, and became her thesis advisor. They worked together closely for almost two years."

"And you suggest they were, ah . . ."

"No, not lovers. I think it's more a case of hero worship."

"And Charvat?"

"Well, Follett is discreet. But I think they are, or were, or were in the process of becoming, in–ti–mate."

"Nobody ever tells me anything."

"Not everything on this ship is your business, Jim."

"That's your opinion."

"You want a list? You'd be surprised what a medical officer—"

"No, life is complicated enough already." He drained off the last of his coffee. "I wonder. Guess I should go say hello to the professor. But I want to leave time for a swim before the afternoon briefing."

"No you don't, Jim. No swim, no palaver. You have time for a three-hour nap."

"Come on, Bones. Stop being a mother hen."

"I mean it. You don't feel it now, but it's going to catch up with you."

"If it were any other situation, I might go along with you. But this is such a routine—"

An intercom crackled. "Captain Kirk."

"In the messroom, Mr. Sulu."

"Sir, would you please come to the bridge? We need your opinion on a possible course change."

"Can it wait, Mr. Sulu?"

"No, sir."

"Coming." He stood. "Try to get a nap on the way up, Bones."

"Better yet, have Spock replace you if it's going to be a long session. He's been in there a day."

"First sign of falling apart, I'll do that." As Kirk walked away, Sulu was paging Andre Charvat.

2

Charvat met Kirk at the turbolift. "Good morning, Captain. Do you know what this is all about?"

"No more than you do, Mr. Charvat. A possible course change." They felt the slight shift as the turbolift changed axes; now headed up rather than forward. "It must have something to do with pure science, since..." The doors parted. Kirk felt an irrational moment of annoyance, that no one was looking at him. Then he saw what they were looking at.

On the main viewscreen, the image of an earthlike planet, almost full phase. Near the middle of the planet was a blue light, bright as a welder's arc.

"What is that, a signal light?"

"Apparently not, sir," Sulu said. "It moves."

"It seems to be the planet's ... sun," Uhura said.

Kirk moved to the command module and sat down, without taking his eyes off the apparition.

"Flatly impossible," Charvat said.

"Yes, sir," Sulu said. "Nevertheless—"

"A star has to have several times the mass of Jupiter, to sustain the feeblest fusion reaction." Charvat's eyes were also riveted to the scene.

"The course change you requested a decision on, Mr. Sulu, was that we delay the mission to investigate this object?"

7

"Yes, Captain."

Kirk snapped out of it and spun his chair around to address Charvat. "Well, Mr. Charvat? It seems strange enough to my layman's eye. Do you think it justifies stopping for a few hours?"

"*Hours,* sir? Days, if it is what it seems."

"Somehow I thought that was what you would say." He swiveled back around and regarded the image again. "I think I had better interrupt Mr. Spock's meditation."

He tapped out a sequence on the buttons on his chair's arm, and they were all treated to the caterwauling that passes for music on Vulcan, Spock's home planet.

"Mr. Spock!" Kirk said, rather loudly.

"Yes, Captain?"

"With apologies for interrupting, I believe we have something on the bridge that you would find very interesting."

"Thank you, Captain. I will join you immediately."

The chair in front of the defense sub-systems monitor was empty; Charvat took a seat. "Mr. Sulu," he said, "what sort of star does this planet orbit?"

"None, sir. It's a rogue."

He nodded his head slowly. "That in itself is remarkable. What is its diameter?"

"A little over eleven thousand kilometers."

"Nearly the size of Earth," he mused. "It must be the largest rogue planet ever found, by far."

"Uhura," Kirk said, "would you check that, please?"

The Bantu woman's slender fingers danced over the buttons of her comm station console, generating a ripple of electronic music and a flat, feminine computer voice: "Catalog."

"Search for largest diameter. Category, rogue planet."

"Searching . . . 946 kilometers, NBD 287, 722—"

"Endit." She looked at Kirk. "You didn't want the number of it, did you, sir?"

"No, uh, just verifying." His brow furrowed as he stared at the thing. "Rogue planets, Mr. Charvat, rogue planets . . . if I remember my cosmology, they're some sort of leftovers. From a star that never became a star."

"Yes sir. If the proto-star's mass is less than, say, a hundredth of the Sun's, random perturbations between fairly large masses can separate them from the general system. Send them out on their own."

"But not with seas and an atmosphere."

"Quite impossible. The lighter elements outgas in a relatively short period of time, so the elements necessary for water and air are absent, even if there were a source of heat."

The turbolift doors slid open and Spock stepped out. He looked at the screen and raised an eyebrow. "Very interesting." He listened for a minute while Sulu and Charvat filled him in. Then he turned to Kirk.

"Captain, have you ordered a biosensor analysis of the planet?"

"Not yet, Mr. Spock. Obviously the planet has life." The land area was mottled green and brown.

"I suggest that in order to solve the cosmological mysteries of this planet, we might initiate a search for intelligent life."

"Mr. Sulu."

"Right away, sir."

Charvat: "Mr. Spock, you mean to say you think that the miniature sun is an artificial construct?"

"It seems probable, by Occam's Razor.* It would

---

*A logical principle ascribed to William of Occam (A.D. 1280–1349): *pluralitas non est ponenda sine necessitate.* Assumptions intake a most unlikely chain of natural events, some of which have never been observed but exist only in theory, to explain the phenomenon.

"Also, the planet itself appears to have been modified by intelligent direction. The coastlines show an unnatural regularity." Though much obscured by cloud, the planet seemed to have two large seas, north and south, with a single land mass in the form of a broad ribbon around the equator. The north and south coasts appeared to be straight lines.

"In a relatively short period of time, geologically speaking, those coastlines would be broken up. To insist on a natural explanation for their regularity requires an unacceptable coincidence between the forces of plate tectonics, ocean currents, and erosion."

"On this side of the planet," Sulu said, "there is no sign of life more intelligent than a low primate. Many different forms of life, but no intelligent ones."

"Interesting. Perplexing. Captain, I would value Dr. Atheling's opinion on this." Kirk asked Sulu to page him.

"It will be the same as mine," Charvat said evenly.

"Very likely," Spock said. "However, since his specialty is nonthermal sources of radiation, he will bring a different orientation to the problem. You and I are thinking in terms of conventional fusion as the source of energy. There may be a simpler solution."

He turned to Kirk. "Captain, with your permission, Mr. Charvat and I will go below to the physics laboratory. We need far more data."

Kirk nodded. "I'll have Dr. Atheling meet you there." The two science officers went down the gangway to the deck below.

---

troduced to explain a phenomenon should not be multiplied beyond necessity. Informally: the least complicated explanation is probably the right one.

Atheling joined Spock and Charvat, after a general meeting had been arranged for 1800 that evening. Kirk decided to take McCoy's advice in two categories: he would catch a few hours' sleep, and the crew was put on "passive standby"—no assignments outside of essential maintenance and security. There wasn't dancing in the corridors, but a lot of shoes were kicked off, a lot of books were picked up. Bunking assignments informally shuffled.

At 1800, ten officers and one civilian met in the briefing room on Deck Six.

James Atheling was a slight man in his early sixties who, like many academics, refused youth-simulating cosmetic drugs. He had sparse gray hair and a face full of character, and affected spectacles whenever he thought a classroom might benefit by a touch of archaic theatricality. This wasn't one of those times; he wore contacts. He kept his hands clasped behind his back, and spoke with quiet emphasis.

"It has to be artificial," he said without preamble, as soon as the last one was seated.

"Without going into the mathematics of it too deeply, let me describe the situation. What we seem to have is a tiny black hole in orbit around the planet. A black hole about the size of a pea.

"As you know, black holes don't shine. The reason they were *named* black holes is because the gravitational gradient at their edge, or 'event horizon,' is so steep that not even the most energetic photon can get out.

"Black holes don't shine, but this one does. This is our evidence for artificiality.

"Amassed around this black hole is a fairly dense cloud of hydrogen and helium. The cloud isn't dense enough, of course, for a fusion reaction to take place. The radiation that comes from the . . . construct is from

11

the kinetic energy of particles falling into the black hole, at nearly the speed of light."

"Beggin' yer pardon, Professor," Scotty said. "That disna' mak' sense—doesn't make sense. It's an unstable situation. The black hole would suck up all its hydrogen and helium an' then joost sit thair. Withoot figures, I couldna' say hoo lang—"

"About ten years," Charvat said. "At the present rate of radiation."

"Which is half of the mystery, Mr. Scott," Atheling said. "It has to be regularly resupplied with hydrogen and helium." He paused to let that sink in.

"As a matter of fact, that wouldn't be terribly difficult, not in theory. We could do it ourselves."

"Bussard ramjet," Scotty said.

"That's right. Early interstellar transports did just that: scoop up interstellar hydrogen and helium to use as fuel." He reached up to touch nonexistent glasses, chuckled. "Sorry. I have a tendency to lecture.

"The bigger mystery is that the darned thing shouldn't exist at all! As tiny as the black hole is, it's far too massive. It should use up all of that gas in seconds; go out in a blaze of glory. But it doesn't. Something is holding the gas back."

"And on the other hand," Charvat broke in excitedly, "something is holding the gas *in!* Otherwise, radiation pressure would disperse the cloud in a matter of weeks."

"Some kind of tractor and pressor fields?" Uhura suggested.

"We thought along those lines," Atheling said, "though it's difficult to see where you would put the field generator."

"What's the problem?" Kirk said. "We use displaced origins as a matter of routine."

"Only in empty space, Captain," Spock said, "or

on the surface of a planet. Geometrically, these fields would have to have their origin at the center of the black hole."

"I see, Mr. Spock. A very non-Euclidean place."

"Well put, Captain." Spock looked at Atheling, who nodded and sat down. Spock rose and paused, looking almost perplexed.

"The next logical step, after our observations and deductions had come this far, was to send an automated probe to the vicinity of the black hole. I did authorize this, Captain, in your absence; such exploration has been done before, and I saw no great risk involved, although admittedly it is an expensive piece of equipment."

"I would have authorized it, Mr. Spock. What you're trying to say is that it dropped into the hole and someone is going to be writing a long report."

"The inspector general will need a report, but no, it did not fall into the black hole. It simply disappeared, approximately two hundred kilometers from the object."

Scotty broke the silence. "Could it hae been tidal stresses?"

"Not at that distance," Spock said. "Neither was it atmospheric friction. The temperature was high, but well within operating limits."

"It was sending complete data one-microsecond," Charvat said, "and no data the next microsecond. We were tracking it excellently. It just disappeared."

"And there's no explanation?" Kirk said.

"None whatsoever," Spock said. "It is our feeling that the answer to these mysteries lies not with the black hole, but on the surface of the planet it illuminates."

3

We've just completed a detailed mapping of the planet Anomaly (so named by Lieutenant Commander Charvat), and have found no artifacts suggesting the planet is or ever was inhabited by intelligent beings.

Much of the land area of Anomaly is jungle, and the planet has a very active, almost Mesozoic, ecology. Its surface and seas are aswarm with creatures man-sized and larger, mostly quite aggressive. So I've selected both the landing site and the landing party with some care.

It was a formidable crew that trooped into the transporter room at 1100. Captain Kirk was leading the team. Then three brawny Security men: Hevelin, Bounds, and Moore. Sharon Follett was along for her dual specialties, astrophysics and xenobiology. They were waiting for Octavio Hernandez, a planetary sciences specialist, who was checking out some special equipment from the armory.

James Atheling had come along to see them off. He and Follett sat on the steps to the unit deck, while the others lounged around the control console.

14

"Sharon," he said, "I don't like the feel of this. I wish you hadn't volunteered."

"Oh, Jim." Her mouth set in a tight line.

"Really. I've been on more planets than you have. Even the settled ones are full of surprises, usually unpleasant."

"Thanks for the lesson, Doctor." He winced. "I'm not your young advisee anymore. At 41 I think I've learned how to take care of myself."

"You're still only two-thirds my age; show some respect. Why didn't you let Charvat take it?"

She laughed. "Andy wanted it, but he couldn't pull rank, not against my xenobiology. This is the third time it's happened."

"You after his job?"

She looked at him sharply. "After a job like his, yes. And Mr. Spock's, eventually. You think I can't do it?"

"Oh, I'm sure you're equal to it. I just wonder whether your ambition might not be clouding your judgment, in this particular case. That's a nightmare of a world."

"In the second place, we have phasers and body armor. In the first place, it's curiosity, not ambition."

"If it were curiosity you could go on the second trip."

She sighed. "There may not *be* one—oh, there's Octavio." The ensign was coming through the door with a frictionless cart loaded down with metal.

She leaned over and kissed him on the cheek. "Don't worry, Jim."

The body armor was like a tightly-fitting suit of fine-mesh chain mail. Sharon found the one tagged with her name, removed boots and tunic, and stepped into it. Once her arms were in the sleeves, the front

15

closed automatically, as if it were zipping itself up, leaving no seam. She squeezed her arm and leg, testing the suit, then hit herself hard in the abdomen. It made a sound like striking wood.

The suit was totally flexible—in fact, felt like silk—so far as the person inside was concerned. On the outside, it was rigid as steel. "See?" she called to Atheling. "If a dinosaur tries to bite me, it'll just get a mouthful of broken teeth." She left her boots and skirt in a locker, then clipped a communicator and a Type II phaser onto the suit.

"Places," Kirk said. The six explorers stepped up and took their places on the circular deck.

"Energize." A familiar warbling sound filled the transporter room, and the people on the deck were enveloped by cylinders of shimmering light.

Otherwise, nothing happened.

Captain's Log, Stardate 6133.6:

Mr. Spock and Dr. Atheling agree that the failure of the transporter to work must be somehow allied with whatever forces allow Anomaly's microstar to exist. At any rate, it's now more important than ever that we investigate the planet's surface.

We will have to go down by shuttle, which is irregular but poses no real problem. I've added one person to the exploration team: Ensign Frost, an engineer and experienced pilot. Otherwise the team and landing site are the same as before.

The shuttlecraft cruised at about a thousand meters, buffeted slightly by thermals from the steamy jungle below. "There it is, Captain,"—the pilot had to shout over the wail of rushing air—"to starboard."

Kirk leaned forward and looked out to his right. "Very good, Ensign." It was several acres of broad savannah, near a wide, slow river. They would land in the middle of the field.

"Pressors, please," the ensign said, and the six passengers activated the fields that would immobilize them for the landing.

It was a soft, flawless landing, the craft touching gently on all three pads simultaneously. But there was an unexpected problem: the savannah grass was taller than a man.

"That's strange," Kirk said as the noise of the engine whined down to silence. "Radar said this grass was only a few centimeters high."

"Sometimes the readings are false, Captain," Hernandez said. "If a wind was blowing across the grass, for instance."

Kirk nodded and rose. Unconsciously following a thousand years of naval tradition—the captain is the last to board a launch, and the first to disembark—he stood in the doorway and palmed the opener.

It was a wall of thick-bladed green grass that smelled like alfalfa. Insect noises. Kirk smiled, maybe reminded of his Iowa boyhood. "Set your phasers on two," he said, and drew his. As he was setting it, he looked back at the others. "I guess—"

The pilot screamed.

In front of Kirk, the grass had parted silently and a meter-wide reptilian head, bright yellow with black eyes and finger-length fangs, peered into the craft for a moment, then lunged.

Kirk threw up his left arm and the creature bit down. It didn't seem distressed by the fact that its fangs wouldn't penetrate the body armor, but held on and tried to drag Kirk away. After three full seconds of stun-level phaser fire, Kirk keeping himself wedged against the doorjamb, the beast finally went limp. Kirk

17

rolled back against the opener and the door whirred shut.

Shocked silence except for the armor's quiet chirring, as Kirk flexed his arm. "Pins and needles," he said. "Must have brushed the secondary lobe—my God!"

Outside, a lumbering tank-sized hairy beast with too many legs had come over to take advantage of the situation. It ignored the shuttlecraft and picked up the front end of the snake-thing, regarded it for a moment, and bit it behind the head, with a mouth so wide it could engulf half the neck.

This revived the serpent, which started to thrash around. It got one coil around the hairy beast (revealing that its body did resemble a snake's, longer than the shuttlecraft, but with wriggling clawed tendrils along the ventral side), but was obviously losing the struggle.

Then a winged thing like a scaly eagle dropped from the sky and fastened itself to the serpent's tail. It chopped once with a beak that resembled a broad-bladed axe, and flew away with a couple of meters of snake meat in its talons. The snake's struggling grew feeble, and finally the hairy monster managed to gnaw through its neck. When the severed head fell, it dropped the rest of the snake, picked up the head, and scrambled away.

Various small animals came, timidly at first, to finish off the job.

"I think we'd better try the alternate landing site," Kirk said. That was a long stretch of deserted beach, some 800 kilometers south-southeast of the primary site; probably less interesting. *Hopefully* less interesting.

They took their seats again and the pilot started flicking switches.

"My pressor field doesn't seem to work," Follett said.

The pilot looked back over his shoulder. "Neither does the engine."

Kirk pulled out his communicator and flicked his wrist to expose the antenna. "Kirk to *Enterprise*."

Louder: "Kirk to *Enterprise*." No response.

He stared at it. "We're in a real jam."

4

<u>Captain's Log, Stardate 6134.2:</u>

This is being recorded by Science Officer Spock, temporarily in command.

We are unable to communicate with Captain Kirk and his team, although they appear to have landed safely, and precisely at the selected location.

It seems unlikely that Captain Kirk would have long remained on the surface of the planet, once it was plain that he could not communicate with the Enterprise. Therefore, either he and the crew are dead or disabled, or the shuttlecraft is unable to lift. When our orbit brings us again over the landing site, Mr. Sulu will determine by biosensor whether they are alive.

Since the translator, communicators, and shuttle engine are mutually independent systems, the probability of all of them malfunctioning at the same time is vanishingly small. The inescapable conclusion is that they have been influenced by some outside meta-system.

"I dinna understan' yer reasonin', Mr. Spock." Scotty was red-faced. The rest of the officers on the bridge pointedly went about their business, or made business for themselves, trying to ignore the gathering storm.

Spock knew enough about human nature not to point out that the commander of a vessel, however temporary, need not explain his decisions to any other officer, not even his second-in-command. He also refrained from any comment about what passes for "reasoning" in humans, as compared to Vulcan logic.

"I should have explained in more detail, Mr. Scott. You wish to lead a rescue expedition, immediately."

"Aye, that's richt." Scotty was trying to stay calm, control his brogue.

"First, it would be illogical to risk lives in order to rescue corpses. Until we know that the team is still alive, there will be no thought of a second mission. My standing orders preclude it."

"Bit—"

"We will know very soon. Second, of all officers of the line, I would be least inclined to risk the life of the engineering officer. The survival of the ship and crew are intimately linked to your special knowledge."

"Sir! *Knowledge* is whit I'm talkin' aboot!"

"In what way?"

He composed his words carefully. "Ensign Frost is a verra guid mon, a guid engineer. I've worked wi' him mony years and ken this. Bit I could pit in ma wee finger whit he kens aboot the shuttle drive system. He's young; the shuttle's gey auld-fashioned ... they dinna teach it so much noo. No' hands-on teachin' —whaur I could tak' it apart blin'fold!"

"This is true but irrelevant. Whatever caused the transporter, communicators, and shuttle to malfunction can have little or nothing to do with spaceship engineering."

"He's yer freen'!"

"He is my commander. I am constrained—"

"Ye're gaun tae leave him there?"

"He would leave me there," Spock said, not defensively, "if the situation warranted it."

"And ye'd want him tae, I suppose."

"Of course. But my wishes certainly would not enter into his decision." Sulu was approaching the command module, with a sheaf of paper. Spock looked toward him but continued to talk to Scotty.

"If the team is alive, there will be a rescue mission. But I will lead it, not you. The situation calls for a generalist. I am a more competent generalist than you are."

Scotty nodded his head slowly. "Ah . . ."

"They are alive, sir." Sulu handed him a printout sheet.

Spock traced down a column of figures with his finger. "Quite so." He continued to look at the sheet. "Up here." He pointed to the upper left-hand corner, where there was a cluster of ones, which became zeros as you worked to the right. "How do you explain this?"

"It's white noise, sir. We get a fraction of a second of it when we calibrate the external sensors for each run."

"This does not happen normally."

"No, sir. But many of our instruments are acting strangely."

"True." He touched a button. "Computer."

"Working," it/she said.

"Biosensor analysis, Stardate 6134.219. Recall data at time of calibration and impose redundancy algorithm. Do the data originate in your systems?"

"No, they do not."

"Does the Lindamood Paradox prevent you from making an analysis of the reliability of the data?"

"Yes. The redundancy algorithm cannot be extended to check the external sensors."

"Assuming the data are correct, how do you interpret?"

"The data indicate that the planet Anomaly is inhabited by a large number of sentient beings, who die simultaneously as soon as the biosensor detects them. Similar data would be generated by a slight potential difference across the sensor array, which might be neutralized by continued operation of the biosensors."

"That seems more likely. Endit." He turned to Scotty. "Mr. Scott, send a work crew out to attach a sensitive voltmeter across the external sensor array. We will do another run and calibrate this white noise with a possible transient potential difference." He punched the comm button. "Deck 19."

"Hangar deck. Ensign Bill Johnson here."

"This is Mr. Spock. Have a shuttlecraft warmed up and ready to launch at a moment's notice. I mean this literally. I will send down a crew immediately."

"Ye'll be gaen doon, Mr. Spock?"

"Not yet. Mr. Sulu, select a crew of volunteers, none above the rank of lieutenant. Stress the peril of the assignment. Outfit them as for a combat operation. They must be in their places, in the shuttlecraft, within one hour. A crew of three will be sufficient; there must be room for the original seven."

"Ye'll no' be aboard, though?"

"Mr. Scott. Please think about the situation. The shuttlecraft is a sturdy vehicle, containing seven days' worth of air, food, and water for seven people. Furthermore, Anomaly has breathable air, and Captain Kirk's people are close to a supply of fresh water. They could survive for more than a month, with proper rationing. Indefinitely, if any of the flora or fauna prove edible.

"The shuttlecraft for which I just arranged will be launched if there is some significant change in the situation within the next 24 hours. If there is none, I will myself lead a rescue operation, with three shuttles and appropriate personnel."

"Combat crew?"

"Certainly not. We have no evidence that violence has been done to the exploration team. The crew will be outfitted for pioneer work—survival—since it seems likely that we may also become stranded."

Scotty rubbed his chin. "Mebbe forever . . ."

"There is a finite probability of that."

5

"Time to try again," Kirk said. The pilot made his hourly check, to see whether the engine would start functioning again spontaneously. This was the eighth try: nothing.

"I guess Mr. Spock's not going to do anything," said Ensign Moore, to no one in particular.

"Don't be defeatist, Mark," Lieutenant Hevelin said. "That won't get us anywhere."

"I'm just being practical, sir, trying to put myself in his place. With our communicators out, he's got no data. He's a Vulcan; he won't commit himself to a course of action without any information to go on."

"I wouldn't worry, Ensign," Kirk said. "He has one datum, from the biosensor: we're still alive."

"Yes, sir. Assuming the biosensor still works." They had checked the tricorder in the shuttle's medical kit, and it was useless.

Sharon Follett had been sitting quietly for a long time, staring out the front windshield. "Captain, I have an idea."

"Yes?"

"Defeatist or not, we ought to plan in terms of the *Enterprise* not being able to help us . . . figure out how to stay alive more than a couple of weeks."

"Certainly," Kirk said.

"Spend the rest of our *lives* here?" Frost said plaintively.

Kirk shook his head. "No, I don't think so. We're only a few weeks away from Academy; Mr. Spock will naturally proceed there. And come back with somebody who can figure this out."

"But it won't do us any good," Follett said, "if we've died of dehydration in the meantime."

She gestured out at the savannah. "See how the wind is building up?" It was a strong, variable wind, whipping the grass almost flat in places. "If we can start a grass fire—"

"Ah!" Kirk stood up. "We'll have what we wanted in the first place." Kirk had chosen the savannah, thinking the grass was short, because nothing would be able to sneak up on them.

Kirk put his phaser on "heat" and carefully opened the door. He pushed the trigger button, aiming at the grass. It should have set everything on fire out to a distance of six meters. But it had no effect. He closed the door quickly.

"Sir," Follett said, "try it on 'stun' again."

He did, and it worked. "That's strange . . . what else do we have that could start a fire?"

"Heating tabs in the food-paks," Frost said.

They wired together a dozen tabs and opened the shuttle door, firing a phaser out into the grass as it opened. Moore ignited the top tab and hurled it out. As the door closed, they could see flames through the greenish-yellow stalks.

For some hours, they'd left the door propped part-way open, for ventilation, by wedging a handbook into the seam. It was soon obvious they'd have to close it completely, or learn how to breathe smoke instead of oxygen.

There was no question that the shuttle could withstand the heat of a brush fire, since it was engineered for the red-hot friction of re-entry. The crew was not so carefully engineered, and soon regretted the fact that the air-conditioning had gone the way of the engine. They stripped off their body armor, and then as much clothing as decorum would allow, and then more. The temperature got to within one degree of the boiling point of water, and then went down as the flames receded. Through the soot-blackened windshield, all they could see was a maelstrom of swirling gray ash.

Frost staggered to the door and pushed the button twice rapidly, jamming the handbook in place. A little ash drifted in, but the air was merely hot, not baking.

"I guess we'd better plan to get some water from the river," Kirk said hoarsely. "I could finish off my week's ration in one gulp."

Captain's Log, Stardate 6134.5:

I dispatched the rescue mission at 1744 today, when telescopic observation of the planet indicated the presence of a forest fire at the landing party's location. The shuttlecraft landed safely, just before nightfall, but again we lost communication with them the moment they touched down.

No further trouble with the biosensor. Mr. Scott's work party did not find the predicted difference of potential across the sensor array, but neither was there a burst of white noise at the beginning of calibration.

The biosensor indicated the usual density of animal life across the surface of the planet, but unfortunately showed no sign of human life at the landing party's location.

They heard the rescue shuttle from inside their own craft, and opened the door to watch it land in the purple light of a spectacular sunset. It touched down about ten meters from them, raising a little puff of ash.

"The ground's cool enough," Follett said. "Should we go out to meet them?"

"Well . . ." Kirk didn't have time to reply. The ash hadn't even settled when the door flipped open and one of the men sprang out. He was ready for anything: full armor, jump harness, Type I ray gun with shoulder stock, a heavy-duty helmet integrated with the armor. The helmet saved his life.

An eagle-like creature even larger than the one they had seen before dropped from the sky and latched onto the man's head, driving him to his knees. He pointed the ray gun up and pressed the stud, but nothing happened.

Another man, standing in the doorway similarly armed, aimed and fired, with the same result. Kirk drew his phaser, still on the low stun setting, and fired. The creature went sprawling, then hobbled up and flew drunkenly away.

"Use your weapons on 'stun'!" he shouted, hearing wings. The man on the ground rolled flat on his back and started firing into the sky. More than a dozen of the flying monsters fell; then the man scrambled up and sprinted for Kirk's shuttle. Inside, he leaned against a chair and panted, hand on his chest, trembling. Freckles stood out dark against waxy skin.

"Birds? Birds," he muttered, then straightened up. "Loo—lieutenant Bill Hixon, Security. Reporting, sir."

"Welcome aboard." Kirk suppressed a smile. Security officers had a reputation for unflappability.

"This is crazy," he said, looking out the door. "Why do they work on 'stun' and not on 'disrupt'?"

"A lot of things don't work on this world, sir,"

Frost said. "Have you tried to restart your shuttle?"

"No . . . is that the problem?"

"One problem," Kirk said. The Security officer shouted across to the other shuttle; they tried and found that their engine was dead, too.

One of the pseudo-birds staggered to its feet. "Tough son-of-a-gun," Hixon said, and showed his admiration by blasting it into unconsciousness again. Then he gave each of the others a dose, for good measure.

"We don't have any lights," Kirk said. "I suppose we ought to wait until morning, to get together and formulate a plan of action."

"Sounds good, sir." Hixon was at the door, staring into the sky and biting his lower lip. "Must be fifty of those buzzards up there."

"You can spend the night with us, if you'd like," Follett offered.

"Uh, thank you, sir, ma'am, but I'd better be getting back to my men. Hey, Alan," he shouted. "You guys want to give me some cover?" The noses of two ray guns poked out of the dark door opposite. The light was fading very fast.

Hixon set this world's record for the ten-meter dash.

As a midshipman, Kirk had learned to sleep whenever there was time: standing up, sitting down, even marching; even when not especially tired, to build up a backlog.

But tonight he couldn't sleep, though his body sang with fatigue and the shuttle chair was seductively comfortable. His mind wouldn't let him: really balled this one, Jim old buddy, they'll melt your medals down and you with them, use it for ballast; any ensign would've seen there was something fishy & sent down an automated probe first; no, you've got to go take a look yourself (Spock is good, though, it's not as if you) left the ship without a commander & put six good people in mortal danger, no, nine now; how many more? five shuttles left, maybe fifteen more, maybe thirty-five, maybe none if Spock . . . stop. If. Spock. Does. The. Logical. Thing.—he'll leave us here & go get help & what should I have done, I should have noted position & taken basic observations & got the hell away from there (but it was just a strange place, not) dangerous; nonsense ecology supports so many large predators, nightmare planet made by some insane God didn't rest seventh day but made this place as a joke. Try to think. If you can't sleep try to think.

The things that don't work, what do the things that don't work have in common & what could make them not work? Transporter, shuttle engine (& airco & lights & tricorder &) but door *works,* head *works.* Phaser, ray guns, only work on low setting & can't kill, what do they have in common? electronics? But the body armor is electronic and it works—must ask Hixon is communicator really dead or only one-way, or is Spock getting a carrier wave or nothing? If Spock thought we were dead he wouldn't have sent a second ship but he has biosensor evidence but our tricorder . . . What do they have in common? nuclear power, tachyon phasing, weak-interactive forces, simple electricity, thermodynamics, disruptor field, what do they have in common? Absolutively nada, put all your physics in a hat and pull out seven or eight pieces of it, here, these things don't work here, sorry, there are more things in heaven and earth, Horatio, than are dreamt of in your philosophy (most misquoted quote in Shakespeare's time "philosophy" meant "science" and that's what we have here) science doesn't work right but not in a consistent way, what do they have in common? Only us, only that it makes things difficult for us, Horatio.

The wind sweet and strong, so strong the very deck boards creak with our progress, hear the rigging hum. Can you make out their name, Mr. Spock? No matter, by her lines she's an American clipper, they must have her colors down for repair. Mr. Sulu, if we could have another point to starboard? thank you. We'll be in hailing distance soon; perhaps they have tobacco or rum to trade. Perhaps news of—what? White smokepuff lost in the wind, boom, splash, shy of our bow. Hoisting black flag, she's a privateer, by God! Yes, Mr. Sulu, I realize we have sail on her and can outdistance her on this line, but we shan't. Mr. Spock, if you would kindly go below and ask Mr. Scott to run out the starboard guns? And Mr. Sulu, we'll have a hard to starboard and strike the mains'l; we'll wait dead for them to come into sure range. I realize we'll heel, Mr. Sulu, do you have a hearing problem? And Mr. Spock, are your boots nailed to the deck? Nevermind, *Ahoy there, Ensign Chekov, and would you have Mr. Scott run out the starboard guns?* There's a good lad, they're all good lads, cheering, but my such language . . .

"Captain Kirk!" Hevelin grabbed his shoulder and shook. "Captain!"

Kirk started to rub his eyes, then snapped awake. "What is it, Lieutenant?"

"Outside." He was whispering.

Kirk shook his head sharply, once. "I don't, uh, things have been moving around out there all night."

"Not things like this. Look!"

31

Look at what, Kirk thought. Can't see anything out of the windshield, oh, the door. He knelt down next to Hevelin and peered through the crack.

In the dim gray predawn light, there were figures moving between the two shuttles. Erect bipeds, stooped, not quite human-looking. Heads too big. Wearing furs, or perhaps covered with hair, not enough light to make out faces. Carrying spears, clubs.

"Shall I stun one, sir?" he whispered.

"No, they're tool-using—what?" They were gone.

"Good runners, too."

"I should say." He stood up. "Well, not much we can do until there's more light. Breakfast?"

"Already had mine, sir. Should I wake the crew?"

"No, I don't mind eating alone." He felt his way to the food rack and virtuously selected one without a heat-tab. Cold chicken and rice. *Better than hardtack with weevils.* Where did that thought come from?

6

From the tracks in the ash between the two shuttles, it looked like a representative of every Anomaly species had come to call during the night. There were marks from pads and claws, from a creature that evidently wore long, narrow track shoes; soft S-curves from the snakes—and on top of all, the four-toed footprints of the humanoids. They had come between the two ships and milled around, but had never come close enough to touch the hulls. Which might be a sign of intelligence.

The bird-things were circling as the tiny sun rose, but there was no other sign of life. Keeping an eye on the sky, Moore stepped out of the shuttle and picked up a small stone. Back in the safety of the doorway, he chucked it at the other craft. It made a satisfying clatter. "That should wake 'em up—"

The door snapped open and all three Security men were there, two kneeling and one standing, guns ready.

"Don't shoot!" Moore said, laughing.

"What the hell, Mark," one of the ensigns said. "We don't have enough trouble?"

"You guys ready to meet?"

"Sure," Hixon said. "We come over there?"

"No, the engineer wants to check out your instruments, sir."

"You cover the sky for us," Hevelin said from behind him. Bounds and Moore stepped outside, phasers ready, scanning the gray wasteland to the jungle's edge.

Kirk walked across at a normal pace, resisting the temptation to look up. The others followed him; there was no trouble.

"Birds seem to have learned from experience," he said. "Frost?"

"Right away, sir."

While Frost was checking out their equipment, to see whether they had the same malfunctions as his shuttle did, most of the others found seats. Hixon and Hevelin sat by the door, low so they could see the sky.

"Lieutenant," Kirk said, "tell me what you know about Mr. Spock's plans."

"Well, sir, we were launched at 1744, as soon as the forest, uh, brush fire was detected. Commander Spock wasn't sure you were alive; you were at too much of an angle for a reliable biosensor reading."

"I wonder why he didn't just move the ship into a higher orbit."

"Sir, there was a work crew on the hull. Our orders, at any rate, were to land if we saw signs of life; otherwise, I was to use my discretion. The *Enterprise* had lost contact with Ensign Frost the moment the shuttle touched down."

"All contact? Not even a carrier wave?"

"As far as I know, sir." Kirk nodded for him to continue.

"Commander Spock figured he could get a biosensor reading on you, and us, by 1930. If we were ... dead, he would proceed to Academy. If we were alive but hadn't returned by 1200 tomorrow, uh, today, he would mount a second rescue mission, and

34

have Lieutenant Commander Scott take the *Enterprise* on to Academy."

"Another shuttle of Security people?"

"No, sir, it was going to be three shuttles of various specialists, and pioneer tools."

"He had the situation pretty well analyzed," Kirk said, and looked thoughtful. "Let's hope the biosensor works."

Hixon nodded, looking up at the birds, and neglected to say "sir." "Be one hell of a trick to survive, with what we've got. For any length of time."

"It would indeed. You haven't seen the half of it." Kirk described the carnage they'd witnessed the day before. "And we have to work our way through a hundred meters of jungle to get to the river."

"Beg your pardon, sir," said the youngest, Ensign Davof, "I don't see that . . . it's that serious. I mean, nine of us with phasers and ray guns—"

"Use your head, Bish," Hixon said. "We'll be here for weeks, months."

"Oh, that's right." He reddened. "The dilithium crystals won't last."

"Not if we're forever blasting our way out of scrapes."

"It's worse than that, Lieutenant," Follett said. "We can't even be sure the crystals are going to last as long as they normally do. We don't know whether they're going to quit on us arbitrarily. Or blow up in our faces. Normal laws of physics don't seem to apply here."

"Sir, I don't understand that," Moore said. "I'm sorry, but it sounds like superstition to me."

Follett laughed. "It isn't. There are well-documented examples of other systems of physics. One's in orbit over our heads: at the event horizon of that black

35

hole, time stands still unless you move it. Distance, though, increases without any . . . effort. Just the opposite of what happens in our corner of the universe."

Moore stared at her. "My brain hurts. Sir."

The two shuttles had enough water stored to last the nine of them nearly eleven days, at normal rations. Their first order of business, though, was to make a trial water run, to find out how difficult their situation was. If they couldn't get to the river, or the water there was tainted in a way they couldn't purify, they would have to go on "shipwreck" rations—which would barely keep them alive long enough for the *Enterprise* to get to Academy and back.

They would wait for Spock; safety in numbers. If he left at 1200, he should land sometime before 1300. By 1245, people were getting nervous.

Hixon was talking to his men, clustered around the door. "Well, we have to face facts," he said softly. "The shipboard biosensor must've . . ."

Faint shrill whistle. To the east, a formation of three shuttles banked toward them. "Here they come, sir!"

They touched down in such a way that the five shuttles formed a rough circle. Spock and eleven others disembarked, while the Security men kept a nervous eye out for trouble.

Along with Spock were four ensigns from the Sciences division, and two from Engineering and Support Services. Dr. McCoy and Nurse Chapel had a shuttle to themselves, which they had outfitted as a miniature hospital and medical laboratory. Lieutenant Uhura had volunteered, as well as Andre Charvat and, surprisingly, James Atheling. Spock and the two engineers had piloted the shuttles.

After general greetings and expressions of relief,

everyone retired to various shuttles. Spock and McCoy joined Kirk.

"It was a relief to see you, Mr. Spock," Kirk said. "Our own tricorders aren't working properly; I was afraid the . . . condition would extend to the *Enterprise*."

"Evidently it did, Captain. Our readings showed no evidence of human life on the planet."

"How did you know we were here? Optical?"

"No; optical resolution was inadequate."

"And no communications?"

"None whatsoever."

Kirk frowned. "You mean to say that you, *you*, embarked on a course of action without any data to back it up? On intuition?" He shook his head. "I didn't know you had it in you, Mr. Spock."

"Logic, Captain, not intuition. A lack of data is not the same thing as no information." He counted off three points on his fingers. "First, it seemed improbable that all of you could have died the instant you landed, since we tracked you to a safe touchdown. If the situation seemed perilous, you probably would have remarked on it.

"Secondly, the only way to stop a communicator from broadcasting a carrier wave is to separate it from its energy unit. It seemed unlikely that all of you would have unplugged your communicators at the same instant."

"We could have been disintegrated. Communicators and all."

"No, not with the shuttle still intact. Three, on the unicellular level, the biosensor readings showed no evidence of any life with an Earth-type chromosomal structure. Even could we posit a situation whereby all of you were killed simultaneously, and in the act of separating the energy units from your communicators,

37

by some process that did not disturb the structural integrity of the shuttle, it seemed absurd that there would not be even one single bacterium left alive."

"You make it sound so easy," McCoy said.

Spock looked at him and raised one eyebrow. "You volunteered for the mission, Doctor. Surely there must have been some thread of logic to support your decision."

"Only intuition, Spock. Worked out the same."

"Whatever your reasons," Kirk said, "I'm glad to see both of you but sorry we put you in the soup." He sat back and proceeded to explain just how thick a soup they were in.

Spock confirmed that their shuttles were in the same shape as the earlier two: all three had tried to keep the engines idling, but they shut down immediately on landing. Nothing in the shuttles worked except altimeter, compass, and door.

In addition to eleven brainy humans and himself, Spock had brought emergency rations sufficient for ten weeks, a large assortment of powered and hand tools, medical and scientific equipment, and a self-erecting survival kit.

The survival kit was a marvel of engineering, about the size of a footlocker. One pull on the lanyard and it would unfold slowly into a hemisphere five meters in diameter. It had an airlock, insulated floor, twenty inflatable bunks, and windows. Properly anchored, it could withstand a hurricane or a herd of angry elephants. It had been used successfully in deserts, jungles, lunar wastes, even underwater.

Unfortunately, when they pulled the lanyard, nothing happened. Since it was supposedly foolproof, there was no way it could be erected manually.

By the time the sun was overhead, the birds had

flown away. They decided to make a foray to the river, to reconnoiter and bring back a sample of water for analysis. Kirk, Hernandez, and the six Security men set out with their phasers and ray guns, and three machetes.

They approached the edge of the jungle cautiously, moving in a "V" formation with Kirk and Hevelin in the lead. Nothing happened until they were about ten meters from the green.

Suddenly a beast like a six-legged cat, lion-sized and glittering with scales, leaped at them from a tree. Three ray guns and two phasers caught it in mid-air; it hit the ground in front of Kirk, inert, and rolled to his feet with a dry rattling sound.

"Good shooting," he said, staring at the stunned animal. It had a long, narrow snout like a barracuda's: jagged tusks protruding over the upper and lower lips.

They saturated the jungle with phaser fire and scanned the tangle of brush for the easiest opening. Huff found it, a trail evidently made by animals on their way from the savannah to water.

They didn't need the machetes. The trail was a meter-wide path of beaten-down, dried underbrush, that evidently got a lot of use. They proceeded slowly, fanning the trail and surrounding jungle with stunning rays. Normally, the range of the phaser was 90 meters, and the ray gun twice that. But it would be foolhardy to rely on that, as Follett had pointed out.

The jungle would have been beautiful, if not for the knowledge of what lay hidden inside it. In the soft light that filtered through the green canopy overhead, flowers exploded in an orgy of vegetable sexuality, from little purple ones the size of buttercups to a shaggy crimson monster two meters in diameter. Even crusty old Hevelin remarked of its weird beauty: thousands of slender red petals spraying from a snarl of finger-thick green-and-white vines. Perfume from the various flowers was like a saccharine icing on the heavy cloying smell of compost rot. In between the intermittent throbbing bursts of phaser fire, the jungle was dead silence.

Just before they got to the water, they had to detour around a huge black bear-like animal, also with six legs. Kirk and Hernandez recognized it as being the type of creature that had made such quick work of the giant snake, the day before. It lay with its eyes open, snoring softly.

The river was slow and wide, pale green with a sandy bottom. They phasered it against the possibility of sea monsters, a strong possibility in the light of recent experience, and Hixon collected a canteen-full of water.

They were equally cautious on the way back, but it wasn't enough.

Huff paused when they got to the huge red flower. Its petals were moving slightly, as if in a gentle breeze. "Hey, look at—" Suddenly he was flat on his back. Three or four strands of green-and-white vine had wrapped themselves around his ankle. He screamed as they pulled him toward the flower, not slowly.

There was a blip of phaser fire, useless, and then Hevelin jumped on top of Huff and chopped at the vines with his machete. Huff rolled free and scrambled back to the path. Hevelin stood, but the vines had him by the wrists. Another snaked out and wrapped around his knee; another found his waist. Somebody was firing a phaser at cyclic rate.

"Stop it!" Kirk said. "That won't do anything!" He waded in toward Hevelin with a machete, but the plant wouldn't let him get near. Tendrils of vine rose up—five, ten, then fifty—weaving in front of him like snakes. One wrapped around the blade of his machete, and pulled it out of his grip.

Hevelin saw what was going on. "Get fire," he shouted in a strong voice, tight with the strain of resisting the plant. "It can't do much against my body armor." It dragged him another step closer to the shaggy flower.

Bounds ran back to the shuttle cluster. Less than a minute after he'd left, Hevelin stumbled and the plant dragged him the last meter. He struggled momentarily and then went limp. The vines fell away and the red flower engulfed his standing form.

As Bounds came sprinting back, he was undoing the top of a large bottle of ethyl alcohol, from McCoy's lab. He hurled it like a bulky grenade; it hit the flower, splashing some petals, and then drained into the bed of vines. He ignited a heat-tab and spun it after the bottle. Before it hit, the alcohol ignited, making a sound like a sudden puff of wind.

Hundreds of vines coiled and uncoiled in a monstrous expression of helpless agony as the pale blue flames danced around its base. The flower convulsed and expelled Hevelin with almost enough force to send him back to the path. Moore reached for his shoulder but the body toppled over, face up.

But it had no face. Moore gasped and fainted dead away.

The flower had eaten through flesh, bone, brain, and body armor indiscriminately, from head to toe, to a depth of about four centimeters. Hevelin looked like a botched autopsy.

Captain's Log, Stardate 6136.6:

Following Commander Spock's orders, we are proceeding to Academy, since he was unable to return from the surface of Anomaly. We may recover subspace communications before then, of course, in which case we will advise Star Fleet Command, and perhaps receive new orders.

As arranged, I computed our escape orbit so that it reached perigee above the landing site, as close as we could come without endangering the Enterprise from atmospheric friction. The physics lab's telescope showed all five shuttles unharmed (at least on the outside), but no crewmen. Four symbols were visible, larger than the shuttles, apparently scraped in the ash:

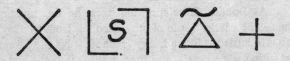

The computer decodes these as meaning "UNABLE TO PROCEED/AIRCRAFTS (SHUTTLES) SERIOUSLY DAMAGED/NOT SAFE TO LAND HERE/SOME CREWMEN or ONE CREWMAN DEAD.

This is from an ancient code used by stranded airmen on Earth. It will be interesting to find out whether this bit of arcane knowledge came out of Mr. Spock's encyclopedic memory, or from Captain Kirk's passion for military antiquities. Assuming we ever see either of them again.

7

Analysis of the water proved it to be drinkable, though they had paid too high a price for the information. They buried Hevelin and made long-range plans.

They needed something more substantial than five shuttles, out in the open, to live in. Especially if their phasers were to give out. There had been three bird attacks in the two days since the initial trouble; single birds who either hadn't got the message, or were trying them out to see whether they were still formidable opponents. No land animals had approached the shuttles during the daytime, but many of them shuffled around at night. One large beast had the annoying habit of banging on the hulls with its head. Of the spear-carrying hominids, there had been no sign.

They decided to build a partially-roofed stockade around the shuttles, and surround the stockade with a moat. Fortunately, all of the power tools worked. Kirk left Hixon and three ensigns with the digger, to start the moat; everyone else headed for the jungle with an assortment of axes and saws—and torches.

They saturated a section of the jungle with phasers on stun and then waded in with torches, looking for plants like the one that got Hevelin. They found two of them: one died a satisfactorily dramatic vegetable death, but the other only sat there and burned. Several other suspicious-looking plants were put to the torch. Kirk finally asked his people to take it easy, lest they find themselves in the middle of a forest fire, damp as the jungle was.

They were in a grove of trees that vaguely resembled birch, with straight trunks 15 to 25 centimeters in diameter, ideal for their purpose. Two Security men nervously walked the perimeter, periodically fanning their ray guns at an unseen host of goblins, while the rest of the crew settled down to lumberjacking.

With a vibrosaw it was ridiculously easy to drop these medium-sized trees. With two quick cuts you made a notch on the side corresponding to the direction you wanted the tree to drop, then just walk around the tree and make a smooth slice through from the other side. One person could drop fifty trees in an hour—unfortunately, there were six people, not one, with vibrosaws, and the problem was not so much getting the trees to fall as keeping out of their way when they came crashing down.

One fell directly on Kirk as he was sidling out of the way of another. It knocked him down, but with the body armor, nothing was hurt but his dignity. He clawed his way out through the branches, prepared to pour wrath all over some hapless ensign, and found Dr. McCoy standing there with the saw and a sheepish grin.

"Sorry, Jim, I got carried away," he shouted over the shriek of the other saws. "Haven't had so much fun in years."

"Fun? Bo—ones . . ."

"Hell, Jim, I yelled 'Timber.' You just didn't hear me."

Kirk threw up his hands in exasperation and decided to leave his budding Bunyans to watch out for each other. He went back to the clearing, where people with axes and vibroknives were trimming the logs. This was fast work, too; logs were piling up in stacks. The slowest part of the process was carrying the logs from the edge of the clearing back to the shuttles. They had a ground-effect cart, but it was worthless: the ground was uneven and the logs made too unwieldy a load. So they had to carry the logs one at a time, two or three people per log.

There didn't appear to be any administrative or command duties lying around loose, so Kirk found an extra vibroknife and helped with the trimming. He'd wrenched his shoulder slightly, clambering out from under the tree, so he decided not to participate in the log-carrying. This turned out to be a lucky decision.

Absorbed in the simple manual labor, lost in private thoughts, it took Kirk a moment to respond when someone yelled *"Hey!"*

He looked up and saw that the warning was directed at two men carrying a log, halfway to the shuttles. They looked back toward the man who was shouting, which was a mistake.

"Look out!" He was pointing.

A cloud of twenty or thirty arrows fell on the men, most of them bouncing harmlessly off their body armor. One man was hit in the forehead, though; slumped to his knees and fell over. The other appeared to be unhurt, but then he reached for his neck and staggered sideways. An arrow had gone completely through his neck.

"Medic! Dr. McCoy!" A half-dozen phasers bleated at the part of the jungle the arrows must have come from, but the range was extreme. An ensign crashed into the brush to go retrieve McCoy.

Hixon and his team had seen what happened, and jumped into the ditch they'd dug, just as a cloud of arrows came their way. Hixon's ray gun howled back at them; one of his men was hit in the hand, but no one else was hurt.

Hixon crawled out of the ditch and yelled in the direction of the logging detail. "Get me a squad, goddamn it—*get* those bastards!" The men who'd been firing jumped up and ran toward him. The sawing had stopped abruptly, and the two perimeter guards came fighting their way out of the underbrush.

Spock was at Kirk's elbow. "Captain, I don't like this. We have no inkling of the natives' evolutionary level—"

"I know, Spock, General Order One." This was the self-determination order; Star Fleet exploration teams were to minimize the effect their technology had on primitive, "developing" cultures. "We've made a hash of it already, just being stuck here." He shouted, "Hixon! Go easy. Observe, don't fight, if possible."

"Yes! Sir!" He obviously didn't think much of the order. Or the Order, for that matter.

Spock and Kirk headed for the wounded men. McCoy caught up with them as they got there.

The man with the head wound was Security's Bounds, trying to sit up, moaning, blood dripping. "Easy there," McCoy said. "Lie down." He sprayed the wound with anesthetic out of his belt kit, and wiped away excess blood. To his surprise, the wound was relatively superficial; the arrow's barb was showing. It had hit his forehead at a tangent, slipped under the skin, bounced off the skull, and slipped out a few centimeters away. He sprayed the wound again and told the man to relax, it wasn't serious.

The other wounded man was in worse shape. The arrow had gone through the center of his throat; blood bubbled at his lips and he was turning cyanotic. Nurse Chapel ran up with McCoy's black bag. The man was trying to say something but only gurgled horribly.

46

"Tracheotomy," McCoy muttered, grimacing. With some difficulty he broke the barb off the arrow and pulled it out. A thin stream of bright blood spurted out, nearly a meter, spattering Kirk's boots. "Aw hell," Bones drawled softly, "got the carotid, too." He took the electronic scalpel the nurse offered. "Lift his shoulders, Jim." Kirk did so, while Nurse Chapel steadied the man's head. McCoy felt for the cricoid cartilage, measured down a knuckle-and-a-half, and tried to start his incision. The electronic scalpel didn't buzz; didn't cut. Bones said a single savage word, and threw the thing away.

Chapel nodded at Spock, who took her place. "Metal scalpels in the bio kit," she said, rising.

"No time," he said, pointing to the vibroknife Kirk had brought over, lying on the ground. "Gimme that." It was crusted with drying sap and dirt.

He turned on the knife and made a slash. Kirk turned his head and tried to think of something pleasant.

"Tube," Bones said. "Okay, clamp for the artery ... go get a couple of stretcher bearers, get set up for surgery. Better send a half-liter of type-O surrogate."

He sighed and sat back on his heels. "He'll be all right, Jim. Probably have a hell of a scar, though. Give you odds the anabolic protoplaser won't work, either."

Kirk braved a look. The man didn't look "all right" to him: eyes rolled back, throat and face a gory mess, blood oozing from the cut Bones had made. "What about Bounds?"

"Oh, he'll be all right tomorrow. Even if I have to stitch it. Some painkillers—"

"Stitch?" Kirk asked.

"That's the way they used to close up wounds," Spock said.

"Needle and thread," Bones added.

Kirk winced. "Think I'll try to stay out of trouble."

47

8

Kirk followed the medical team partway back to the shuttle. Suddenly there was a commotion at the jungle's edge.

"We got one," Hixon shouted. Two of his Security men were carrying the limp body of one of the humanoids. Another carried a strangely-shaped bow.

Following some obscure instinct, they carried the creature to the middle of the circle formed by the partly-dug moat. Kirk sent for Sharon Follett, who was inside the medical shuttle, helping set up for surgery.

"Doesn't look so human in the light," Kirk said. Its arms and legs were too long, and had extra elbows and knees: limp, it looked like an abandoned marionette. The hands and feet seemed identical, but not like a monkey's. Four long digits with extra joints and no nails.

The most striking thing, though, was its head—more accurately, the lump where its head would have been if it were a human being. It had no eyes, nose, or ears; just fur.

Kirk remarked on this as Follett came up. "Well, Captain, let's see." She knelt by the head and gently probed, moving the fur around, speaking to no one in particular. "Some dogs don't seem to have . . . strange. Hmn. Maybe it sees through its . . . mouth. . . ."

Someone laughed nervously. "I've seen stranger things," she said, prying its mouth open.

It had neither tongue nor teeth. Just a hardened gum ridge and a gullet. "Odd. Get outa my light." Spock had been hovering over her; he stepped back.

"No vocal apparatus, as far down as I can see. Nothing like salivary ducts or . . . digesting mucus." She looked up at Spock. "You know, like the Krovill." Spock nodded thoughtfully. That was an animal on Vulcan, toothless, but able to eat anything from an artichoke to a xylophone.

She squeezed its arm—"Muscular"—and turned it over, then rolled it on its back again. She sat back on her heels and gazed at it, frowning.

"I don't know what to make of it, Captain. It shouldn't be able to exist."

"You mean because it, uh, it doesn't . . . "

"That's right. It doesn't have any obvious organs of generation or excretion. And the mouth opens into what looks like nothing more than a breathing tube."

"Perhaps it isn't truly representative of its species," Spock said.

"Possibly . . ." Follett said. "It could be a drone, like a worker bee, and not necessarily need to reproduce. And there are animals that go through a terminal stage of life, where they don't eat."

"The species Lepidoptera, on Earth," Spock said. "Some of them only feed as larvae."

It moved. "Get back!" Hixon said, and gave it a short stunning burst.

Follett picked herself up and brushed away dirt. "Mr. Hixon. I don't think the creature is that dangerous, under the circumstances."

"Maybe not," Hixon grumbled. "Sorry if I startled you, Lieutenant."

She ignored him, already absorbed in studying

the creature again. "It's too large and complex, Mr. Spock. Not like a drone bee or a butterfly. Wish we had a tricorder."

"Should we tie it up?" one of the Security men asked. Hixon looked to Kirk.

"No, I don't think so. We—we can all be excused for not sticking strictly to General Order One, at least in the sense of violating it passively or in self-defense. But we can't take this being prisoner."

Spock nodded. "We have to assume that its use of tools implies intelligence. Even though there do exist habit patterns—instincts—quite as complicated as aiming and firing a bow."

"You mean we have to put it back where we found it? Sir?"

"That's right," Kirk said. "Without the bow, I think. No sense in asking for trouble."

"Can't dissect it," Follett said. "Can't set up behavioral experiments . . . ah!" She stood up. "I can get a sample of hair, at least."

While she ran back to her shuttle for scissors and a container, Spock inspected the creature closely.

"Mr. Spock," Hixon said, "how can it get along without eyes? How could it possibly use a bow and arrow?"

"It *is* interesting," Spock said, re-checking the head. "Not without precedent, though. On the planet Babel there is a creature—in English you would call it a 'mind-toad'—that has no organs of sight, hearing, or smell. It detects its prey telepathically, and kills it with a well-aimed jet of saliva, which contains a nerve poison.

"It seems likely that the organism responsible for Lieutenant Hevelin's death has a similar talent." Follett came back; he watched as she snipped hair from the creature's arm, head, and hand, putting each in a

50

separate vial. "As Lieutenant Follett would verify," he continued, "the first rule of xenobiology is caution. We really know very little about the various ways things can live, and cannot afford to generalize."

She nodded. "There are rocks that have the properties of life, and vapors, too. There are things that live only for minutes, long enough to feed and reproduce; others that seem only to die by accident. No rules.

"I guess you'd better be taking it back."

Two of the Security people picked it up, arms and legs, while Hixon drew his ray gun and checked it. "Caution, Spock, not just in the intellectual sense," Kirk mused. "If a flower can reach out and—"

Suddenly all hell broke loose. The creature came suddenly awake and kicked itself free. Its foot reached out and snapped the ray gun from Hixon's grasp: it held it properly, depressed the trigger, and fanned it in a full circle, waist high.

Kirk felt the sudden cold shock and slumped to the ground, tingling. He watched the creature drop the ray gun and run away. Its speed was incredible; it crossed the two-meter-wide moat as if it weren't there.

Time passes very slowly when you're stunned. You feel sleepy and very uncomfortable; colors are lurid and painful, but close your eyes for a second and you'll lose consciousness. Kirk kept his eyes open and tried to grit his teeth, but of course his jaw muscles wouldn't cooperate. He lay there and waited for the tingling, pins-and-needles sensation in fingers and toes, that would mean it was wearing off.

Hixon, the largest, would probably recover first. He couldn't move his eyes, but one of the man's hands was in his field of vision. He stared at it, wondering whether anyone had escaped the ray.

Maybe McCoy and Chapel, insulated by the hull of the shuttle. But the door would be propped partly

51

open, for ventilation. He had complained about that, unsanitary. If they weren't in the line of sight of the door, they'd be all right. But they wouldn't know that anything was wrong. Unless they heard the scuffle. But they were concentrating on, what's his name, Ensign Huff, with the throat cut open. Needle and thread.

There. Hixon's hand twitched. And somebody is up and around, there's his shadow.

A huge silver bird.

It walked cautiously among the fallen humans, looking left and right, sometimes spreading its wings with a curious scraping sound. When it opened its beak it made a noise like an electric arc. It smelled of lilac.

Kirk watched it straddle the still form of Sharon Follett. It raised its head and came driving down with the axe-like beak, right into the small of her back. Beak hit body armor with a loud *crack;* the bird flapped and screeched.

Kirk's fingers and toes began to hurt. He would recover in a few minutes.

The bird began to probe Sharon Follett's body with its beak, gently, looking for a soft place. When it found her neck . . . Kirk remembered the snake.

Another shadow. Kirk still couldn't move his eyes. The bird stopped searching and stared at the intruder.

It was Hixon, staggering, almost recovered. He had the ray gun but couldn't raise his arms. He shouted at the creature, an inarticulate roar. The bird stepped away from Sharon and began to circle, wary, wings spread, head tucked in.

Kirk could move his head. Painfully, he craned around to look at Hixon. He was holding the ray gun in both hands, trying to raise it.

Suddenly the bird rushed him, wings crashing. It

grabbed him by the shoulders and beat for the sky. Hixon dropped the gun. Helpless, Kirk watched them raise off the ground, two meters, three—

Off to his left, a phaser warbled. Bird and man crashed to the ground. The bird shook itself and flew away. Hixon had landed on his head, and lay still.

It had been McCoy. He was staggering some, but obviously hadn't been hit as hard as the others. He kneeled by Hixon, checked him out, and then said something in a low voice.

Kirk tried to call out and surprised himself with three intelligible sounds: "Is . . . Hix . . . on?"

McCoy worked his way over to him, walking like a very old man. "He'll be all right. What the hell happened, Jim?"

"They, they caught . . ." Kirk clamped his teeth together and tried to work the numbness out of his jaw. He rolled over on his side, facing McCoy. "They caught one, one of the humanoids. Either he was playing possum or the stun ray wore off instantly. He took the ray gun from Hixon and used it on us. Got away."

McCoy squinted up into the sky. "More birds coming. Can you use a phaser yet?"

"No, my arms . . . can you give me a stim shot?"

"Love to. Hypo spray doesn't work, though. And the oral stimulants we've got are for fatigue, not—" He aimed and fired; a bird fell some distance away. "Not this."

He stood up. "Nurse Chapel ought to be up and around; I could move after seven minutes. I'll get her a phaser and we'll stand guard until—"

"What about Huff? Aren't you operating?"

"No." He was walking back toward the shuttle and didn't turn around. "While Nurse Chapel and I were stunned, his lungs filled up with blood."

53

They couldn't finish the stockade that day, but did manage to widen the moat to four meters and move all of the timber inside. They buried Huff at dusk.

Kirk sat with Spock and McCoy in a darkening shuttle.

"Quite a day," Kirk said, and quoted the Chinese curse: "We live in interesting times."

If Spock recognized the quote, he didn't mention it. "Yes. In view of the conditions here, two casualties is not an unreasonable toll. Regrettable, but it could well have been much worse."

"Besides," McCoy said, his voice hoarse with fatigue, "they were only humans."

"Bones! That's uncalled for."

"I know. Sorry, Spock."

"Dr. McCoy's attitude is understandable. But ill—"

"Illogical, yeah. No, it's not so much Huff dying under my care; I've lost patients before. I've lost them when it was my own fault, not some monkey with a ray gun.

"What bothers me is two casualties in two days. What happens tomorrow and the next day ... two more? And the next ten weeks? When the *Enterprise* comes back, there won't be anyone left for Scotty to rescue."

"Always the ghost at the banquet, Bones." He tried to change the subject. "Why did you bring Dr. Atheling along?"

"He volunteered," Spock said, "and he made it clear that his request had the force of an order."

"You let civilians order you around?" Bones said.

Kirk chuckled. "He's a commodore, Bones. Reserve grade, but a commodore nevertheless—has to be, in order to be dean of a Star Fleet college."

"Crazy world, Academy."

"I realize, Captain, that I could have denied his request. I would have gone before a board, but ample precedent does exist."

"Well, he was working as hard as anybody today, considering his age," McCoy said. "I better talk to him tomorrow. If he gets a hernia or a slipped disc, he's going to stay hurt a long time."

"I didn't mean to criticize his willingness to work," Kirk said, "and I appreciate his not pulling rank on *me*—but I just don't see what good an expert on— what was it?"

"Nonthermal sources of bosons and tachyons."

"—that sort of thing, what good it will do us here. I'd rather have a young ensign who grew up on a jungle planet." He sighed. "We can never tell, of course. I suppose I should be glad that he wanted to help."

"I don't think 'helping' was uppermost in his mind, Jim. I think his interest in Lieutenant Follett has become more than, um, avuncular. He couldn't let Charvat be the knight in shining armor." He cleared his throat. "No, that's unkind. I don't think it's a matter of jealousy. He cares for her. She's in trouble.

"Same reason I had to leave an ensign in charge of sick bay. Nurse Chapel wouldn't be here if you were safe aboard the *Enterprise,* Spock."

He answered with a stony silence.

"Sorry." The chair creaked as he stood up. "The tireder I get, the harder it is to keep from saying what I mean. Bid you gentlemen good night."

Bones took off his body armor and boots, then stretched out on a stack of food boxes, using his boots and shirt for a pillow. He listened for a while to Kirk and Spock, and then dozed, half awake:

Bloody nightmare and not the last one, *Doctor,*

see now why you had to study that stitching up cadavers—terrible but at least they didn't bleed. Who's
gonna stitch *you* up, Georgia boy? She's a damn fine
nurse & a better scientist than you, but she never
sewed up no cadavers, no suh.

He's more upset than he wants us to know, Jim
just said, sorry Jim, this is outa your league.

All gonna die, this is not a planet it's a goddamned symbol, grim reaper get us all. Pre-med psych
they told us we wanted to be doctors because we had
an abnormal fear of death, abnormal? He was so
sure . . .

Chapel held up real good, looked white but never
shook or flinched, not used to this kind of butcher
shop, never was ER resident Atlanta General, boy come
in once his neck . . .

Foo. Gotta stretch supplies. Half the inventory's
useless here. More'n half; we're back in the twentieth
century, twenty-first? When did they get electronic
scalpels and DNA match synthesizors? Who cares,
we're gonna run out if people don't watch their step,
can't do surgery every day . . .

Old Atheling, well, he's not so old. When was
the last time, *Doctor,* you were willing to give it all up
for a woman's love, give anything up? Not while you
were married, not since, it was little Sara with the big
eyes (can't even remember her last name) summer
and fall on the Outer Banks salt & sweat & you left
when the mosquitos came, she stayed, you only lost
one trimester, cold bastard, what Honey said when she
left with, where is Joanna now? you don't even know
what planet your own daughter's on. Yet I do love her
in my own . . .

Midair collision son-of-a-bitch was too jazzed to
even start the flyer God knows how he got around the

ignition, would've had to build a new face even if I could've fixed his heart . . .

Went wrong even before we got married . . .

How does it go? Cooks cover their mistakes with mayonnaise, lawyers cover their mistakes with words, doctors cover their mistakes with dirt. But the first one is, ninety seconds earlier & I could have saved him, or if he'd been younger . . .

You could charm the shoes off a snake they said, and Honey was a real challenge but then you wake up married & don't like each other any more than you have to & have a baby to make it work—dumb?

Second day on the job & you get open-heart surgery at three in the morning, guy's crushed to a pulp & lost most his blood by the time they roll him in, know he's a goner with the first tricorder reading, ambulance crew glad to be rid of him you hear them joking while they wash up, on old Olympus' . . .

How many have you lost, *Doctor,* you lost count early, how many women have you lost? the same number you charmed the shoes off, on *Mount* Olympus', long day ahead . . .

She would care if she knew, last letter was from Aries, *Ant*ares. Auditories, glosso-pharyngeal, I do love her flowering tops, get some sleep so . . .

On Mount Olympus' flowering tops, a fat-assed German ate some hops: Olfactory/optic/motor oculi trochlear/trifacial (a fat-assed German) abducent/facial/auditory/glosso-pharyngeal, an old Olympus' on *Mount* Olympus' . . .

"Bones?"

"Sorry, Jim. Talkin' in my sleep."

9

They lost another one that night: Hixon. No sign of any violence; nothing but an open door and an empty bed.

"I don't understand it either," McCoy was saying. Hixon had torn a neck muscle in his fall, so Bones had worked on him with tape and an inflatable brace, then given him sedatives and let him sleep on the operating table. "You couldn't wake him up with a sharp stick."

"I wonder," Kirk said. He peered into the makeshift operating room. "Could he have gotten disoriented? Opened the door and wandered away?"

"He should've been out cold for 18 hours. Unless I screwed up the dosage, which I don't think—"

Kirk cut him off with a wave of the hand. "Could one of those creatures have carried him away, without waking him up?"

"Sure. Could of *dragged* him away—but Jim, to do that, they'd have to figure out which shuttle had the unconscious person in it, sneak in, figure out how to open the door . . ."

"Well, that's not hard. Push the silver button."

"Wouldn't be hard for you or me to figure out. Didn't see any silver buttons on the trees I was cuttin' down."

"And they could have watched from the jungle . . ."

"Oh, come on. You've got General Order One on your brain; use some common sense. They're primitives—tips of those arrows were bone splinters. Show 'em a button and they'll try to eat it."

"Bones, sometimes you—"

"Captain!" Ensign Ybarra ran up. "Footprints, in the moat." They followed her back to the shallow trench.

"Look like his," McCoy said. Heavy dew during the night had softened the prints people had made the previous day. Hixon's footprints were sharp and deep, and probably from the largest boots on the *Enterprise*.

McCoy shook his head. "It can't be. I remember counting out three pills—most people get two, but he's big and I wanted to be sure he slept deep and long. I did give him three."

"Evidently he didn't take all of them," Kirk said.

"I watched him. Besides, what reason—"

"There's an explanation, Doctor." Spock had been walking around with them, but hadn't said anything until now. "You gave him what would have been a proper dosage under normal circumstances—"

"Damn!" Bones slapped his fist into his palm. "Physics doesn't work on this planet; you can't expect chemistry to."

Ensigns Moore and Davoff walked stiffly up to the three. "Sir," Moore said to Kirk. "Request permission to form a search party."

Kirk chose his words carefully. "I appreciate Security's long tradition of . . . mutual support. But under the circumstances, I don't think there is any chance that Lieutenant Hixon can have survived—alone, unarmed, and injured."

"Yes, sir, we understand. But we can't abandon him."

"You're asking me to allow you to risk your lives, searching for his body."

"If it comes to that, sir. Ensign Bounds has also volunteered."

"*I* forbid that," McCoy said. "I put Bounds on 48 hours' light duty. Besides, he couldn't wear a helmet with his bandages in place."

"Yes, sir." He looked at Kirk.

He thought about it. "I'm not going to let you two do it alone. If you can round up six volunteers, all right—*but!*—you go no further than 100 meters into the jungle, in Hixon's direction of travel. You spend no more than thirty minutes. We do have a job to do, here."

McCoy gave him a dirty look. When the ensigns were out of earshot, he muttered, "Don't say it, Bones."

"I was just going to say I wouldn't have your job on a bet. Let's get some breakfast."

They found their six volunteers, including Uhura ("Not much work for a communications officer around here, Captain."), who led the search party. They did find broken underbrush where Hixon had evidently entered the jungle, which surprised even Moore and Davoff. They'd had to use phasers twice before they got to the jungle's edge, in broad daylight. They found another bootprint some ten meters into the brush, in damp clay at the edge of a trail. Uhura pointed out that the even depth of the print probably meant he'd been walking; running, the toe would have sunk in deeper.

But there was no other sign. In a half-hour they returned.

Kirk stationed the three security men around the

circle, with ray guns, and sorted out the rest of the crew into work parties.

The plan had been to fill the moat with sharp stakes, to discourage a rush from either the natives or the large fauna. But at about two meters' depth, Hernandez struck water. He tried to keep digging, pushing the machine around in the ditch, spraying everybody with water and mud. When the water got halfway to his knees, he scrambled out. The moat filled up.

James Atheling was sitting on the bank of the moat, sharpening stakes, when the water began to rise. He watched it with fascination. "Impossible," he said. "If the water table were that high . . ."

"At least it's working in our favor for a change," Kirk said. "Won't have to go through the jungle for water."

They lashed together a bridge, three logs wide, and got everybody inside the moat. Charvat and the science team went to work on a simple drawbridge arrangement while the other fifteen worked on raising the walls.

The basic structure of the stockade was finished well before dark. Captain Kirk decided that was enough work for a day; tomorrow they'd roof it over and figure out what to do with a couple of hundred sharpened stakes.

McCoy put a few liters of the water through a purifier (it was slightly muddy) and pronounced it good. Unpurified, it was all right for bathing; he rationed out soap and made up a schedule. Four people at a time, two guarding while the others bathed. Together with the three guards stationed on platforms along the inside of the stockade wall, it should be safe enough. And a welcome relief after a day of hard, dusty labor.

The four women went first—McCoy's old-fashioned chivalry—and the others lounged around in small groups, talking, enjoying the security of the new wall. McCoy wandered back into the medical shuttle, and found Spock there, leaning over the field microscope.

"Find anything interesting?"

"Yes." He looked up. "The creature's hair is perfectly round in cross-section. Perfectly round; no variation. The same for all three samples."

"That *is* odd." He studied the image for a moment. "Hardly looks real. Has Lieutenant Follett said anything about it?"

"I don't believe she's had an opportunity to examine the specimens. I made up the slides myself."

"Well, we'll talk to her when she gets back." They stepped outside, where Spock could stand up straight.

On the other side of the wall, the women were giggling and splashing. Spock listened to it and nodded. "If you have a moment, Dr. McCoy, I've been meaning to ask you about something you said last night."

"Go ahead." He sat down with his back against the shuttle.

"You said that you felt Nurse Chapel would not have come down to the planet's surface if I were not here. The implication being that she was concerned for my safety."

"That's right. I think it's obvious."

"Perhaps. Perhaps to you." Spock also sat down, and stared off into the distance. "I don't pretend to be an expert on human emotion, least of all where it is touched by human sexuality."

"Understandable." Because of his Vulcan blood, Spock's own sex life was about as interesting as a stone's, except for a brief period of extreme enthusiasm, every seven years or so.

"I'm not blind to this . . . affection; in fact, I tried

to talk to Lieutenant Chapel about it, last year. She would not discuss it."

"Hm. I can imagine."

"It occurs to me that our situation here, isolated together for some months, might become difficult. But as I say, I am not an expert. I would appreciate your advice."

McCoy thought for a few moments, and then surprised himself with his honesty: "Spock, asking my advice about that is like asking a deaf person about music."

"You're too critical of yourself. In the first place, no one on the *Enterprise* could possibly know Nurse Chapel as well as you do. In the second place, you have a great deal of professional training in human psychology. Your commission—"

"Yeah. Charges me with responsibility for the emotional as well as physical well-being of the crew. But you can take that with a big lump of salt—Spock, some areas of human psychology can't be quantified; can't be approached analytically. The amorphous phenomenon or group of phenomena that we lump under the word 'love,' well, it's the worst of the lot. You need a philosopher or a poet; I'm just not qualified." He didn't mention having flunked his final exam.

"You can advise me, though, in the area of human sexuality."

McCoy tried not to grin. *Can't believe this is happening.* "Sure. Think I remember what it was like."

"Nurse Chapel certainly is aware of our physiological differences, and she appears to be a normal human female. Why does she so actively seek a situation that would result in a lifetime of near-abstinence for her?"

"Beats the hell out of me . . . but you should know more about that than me. Your own mother is human."

"Mother and I have never discussed this frankly."

"That's the most human thing I've ever heard you say." He thought. "Let me put it this way. Sex is only the most visible part of human love, and it's a part that at least superficially yields to analysis—how often, with whom, and so forth—so it's easy to see how, um, an objective observer like yourself would exaggerate its importance.

"But it probably doesn't loom very large in the attraction that Nurse Chapel feels toward you. Women, as well as men, are attracted by power; you hold the second most powerful position on the *Enterprise*. They are attracted by intellect; yours is as prominent as your ears. They are attracted by fairness—yours is congenital—and comforted by behavioral predictability, which you have in spades.

"But most important, in your case . . . women are attracted by the strange, the unusual—and if you don't mind me saying so, you're 'bout as strange as a whistling fish!"

Spock nodded soberly. "I am aware of most of this; I have read human poems, novels, and plays in abundance. Let me ask you for a concrete opinion."

"Shoot."

"I have devised two scenarios, based on the logic implicit in works of fiction. First, it seems obvious that my own lack of response does nothing to discourage Nurse Chapel; on the contrary, it seems to make her even more determined."

"That makes sense. We're perverse that way."

"So perhaps if I were to appear to be affected by her, and make the proper romantic responses . . . then she would lose interest."

"Huh-uh. That might work in a French comedy. In real life you'd wind up with her hanging from your neck like an amulet."

"That is a sensible prediction, I think. The other scenario is more complicated, as it requires a third person. Transference. I would ask another male to take my place in her affections. Someone who is reasonably close to her; someone who knows human nature well. You, Dr. McCoy."

Bones stared at him, then laughed. "You want me to, to *seduce* Nurse Chapel? To take the heat off you?"

"For her own good. Really, Doctor, it's her problem, not mine."

On the other side of the wall, the women laughed, as if on cue. "But . . . but, Spock . . . oh, hell. How can I explain? Chapel isn't . . . Chapel's my professional associate. That she's female is an irrelevant accident. I'm her adviser; a father-figure, if anything."

"Incest taboo?"

"Hell, what have you been reading? There might be some element of that on some naive level . . . but the main thing is, goddamn it, she's not a woman, *she's a nurse!*"

A couple of people turned their heads to see what the shouting was about; McCoy continued more quietly. "Besides, it wouldn't be honest—there are times, I know, when honesty is contraindicated. But leading a girl down the primrose path . . ."

"I wouldn't ask you to do anything against your nature, Doctor McCoy."

"And what the hell is *that* supposed to mean?" McCoy was a little jumpy about the subject, but not because of Chapel. In spite of (or maybe because of) the obvious competition from Charvat and Atheling, Bones was setting his sights for Sharon Follett.

Spock was forcing him to think about it consciously for the first time. Why, indeed, Follett rather than Chapel? Well, Follett was ten years older (four

65

years younger than Bones), and so he didn't have to feel like he was cradle-robbing. Like him, she'd had a short marriage, ending with divorce. Both of the women were advanced enough professionally that he could feel comfortable with them, socially and intellectually; both of them were beautiful women—but Follett's beauty had a hard edge to it.

And there was a factor he could hardly articulate; one he would never try to explain to Spock. Having peered and poked at ten thousand bodies in various states of disrepair, nearly half of them female, he could fairly claim that he knew as much about what makes women tick as did any male within a hundred light years.

But there are various kinds of knowledge. What was involved was the mirror image of the logical axiom that had brought Spock to the surface of Anomaly— that an absence of data is not the same as no information. A surfeit of data, on the other hand, may not dispel a mystery.

And for several years, whenever that mystery has presented itself to Bones, Nurse Chapel has been at his elbow, to preserve decorum and aid in communication. So his private image of her is of a chaperone, hardly a potential lover. And it suddenly occurred to him that her personal image of him couldn't be particularly sexy, either.

"Never work, Spock. We just—" A scream outside cut him short.

Spock and McCoy were the last ones to the door; by that time the bridge was lowered and people were starting across.

About twenty meters away, Hixon walked slowly toward them. His ears and nose had been removed. His eyelids hung slack over empty sockets. He smiled.

10

Chapel had dressed hastily and was waiting for McCoy as he and Spock helped Hixon into the med shuttle and onto the bed. They rolled the bed around to take maximum advantage of the fading light.

"Incredible." McCoy gently touched the smooth skin where Hixon's nose and ears had been. "It's brutal, but . . . where's that magnifier, nurse?"

She handed it to him and he made a closer inspection, and shook his head. "Incredible."

"Does it look like a protoplaser?" she asked.

"No, there's no fusion. Nor granulation. Pores and hairs . . . it's as if he'd been born this way." Hixon continued to smile, not reacting to the examination.

"Could it be a graft?"

"Not in so short a time. But we can check." He and Chapel undressed the patient; there was no place on his body from which skin could have been recently taken.

McCoy pulled at an eyelid, but it was sealed. "I don't know. Any good surgeon could duplicate this, given time and the proper tools. If he had a sadistic streak. But—"

"Don't worry about me, Doctor." Hixon spoke in a slow, strong voice. "I am happy. We'll talk tomorrow. Now I have to sleep."

Chapel broke the silence. "He knew it was you."

"Wouldn't be hard to figure out." He took a field stethoscope out of a drawer. "What gets me is how he managed to . . ." He leaned forward, listening. "Heart stopped!"

Bones put the heel of his hand on Hixon's sternum and pushed hard, then shifted around so he could put all of his weight behind it.

Hixon shook his head slowly and raised a hand. "No. It's all right. I have to sleep."

His heart was still beating, but only three times a minute. He breathed, one soft sigh, about every other minute. They watched over him until it got dark.

Talking in Kirk's shuttle, they came up with a list of strangenesses:

The sentries swore they hadn't been derelict in their duty. They spotted him about the same time as the people bathing did—which meant he must have covered a hundred meters of ground in seconds; there was no way he could have sneaked up on them.

He'd walked as if he could see. He'd been heading straight for the drawbridge when they rushed out and started to guide him.

When he talked to somebody he "looked" at him.

To these things, Bones added a number of medical improbabilities. Then he went back to the med shuttle, to sleep on the floor by his patient; keep him from wandering off again. He dreamed of naked faceless people, two of whom might have been Chapel and Follett.

When he woke, Hixon was sitting patiently on the bed, hands folded in his lap. Bones dressed and opened the door, flooding the cabin with light.

Hixon's body was covered with black stubble. His

hands had only four fingers apiece. Where the thumbs had been, not even stumps. "Good God," Bones said, and Hixon made a sound that might have been a laugh.

"Can you hear me?"

"No-o." His voice was deeper and slower than the day before.

For once in his life, Bones was at a loss for words. "Uh . . . I don't . . ."

"Can you hear me?" whispered a voice inside his skull.

"What?" He glanced at the sky and poked his head out of the door. All of the other shuttle doors were still closed. "If this is telepathy, let me go get Spock."

"I suppose it's a kind of telepathy. But don't bother. I'll call him."

McCoy leaned against the wall and stared at Hixon. "What do you mean, 'a kind of'? You don't move your lips and I hear something inside my head."

"Please. Explaining is tiring. Not so tiring as talking would be, but let me wait and only do it once."

"You don't talk like Lieutenant Hixon."

"I am not Hixon any more." His hands fluttered in a fluid, strangely girlish gesture. *"And your own mind supplies the words."*

McCoy heard the door to Kirk's shuttle slide open. "What's going on over there, Bones?"

"Captain Kirk, Spock; everyone. Please look outside." Hixon slipped off the bed and walked to the door.

Bones put a hand on his arm. "Wait—the sentries—"

"Don't worry." Outside, incredibly, logs and poles floated in the air. They arranged themselves into a lat-

tice roof over the stockade and settled into place, all in a few seconds. Kirk had reckoned it to be at least a two-day job.

"It's safe now. Come on outside."

He stepped out and Bones followed him. "How did you do that?"

"With help." They walked to the center of the circle and waited. Kirk and Spock were on their way; most of the others stood at open doors and gawked at the sudden roof and Hixon.

"Can you read our minds?"

"Only a little, very faint. Spock is clearest. The rest of you don't know how to think of one thing at a time."

Spock was talking to Kirk as they approached. "—no, not like mind-melding at all. It's only on one level, and causes no strain." He fell silent, studying Hixon's changed body. "It's just conversation, without sound."

"That's a relief," Bones said. "I was afraid it was something complicated."

"It probably *is* very simple," Kirk said, "at least from his point of view."

"Simpler than trying to talk, yes. But not as simple as speaking with my own kind."

"You mean that literally?" Bones said. "You consider yourself one of them?"

"I sense your disgust. You feel that 'they' have mutilated me and taken my mind prisoner. I feel sorry for you. What they have done is make me alive for the first time. Born."

"Come on now. You don't miss being able to see, hear, smell? Even though you can get around—"

"Let me try to make you understand. When you see an object, your eyes sense light reflected from or generated by that object, in a very limited range of

70

frequencies. This gives you some idea of the form and composition of the object, at least on the side facing you.

"When you hear a sound, your ears sense that some object nearby is vibrating, again in a limited frequency range. The ears lack the eyes' discrimination, and are easily fooled.

"The sense of smell is trivial. It tells you that there is a substance nearby that is more-or-less active chemically. It lacks even the ears' directionality.

"Neither have I the senses of taste or touch. Touching something tells you where it is, and indicates its texture, at least where you are in contact with it. I know these things directly. And the only practical use of taste is to warn you of dangerous food. I no longer eat."

"What do you do for energy?" Kirk asked.

"I can't answer that directly; human languages don't have the words." He paused. *"There is a word in Vulcan that expresses one basic idea: arivne."*

"It's a religious term," Spock said, "expressing interdependence, or even unity, between matter, energy, and thought."

"Yes, and it gives a true description of the universe, as far as it goes."

"That's not so foreign," Kirk said. "We know that matter can be changed to energy, and vice versa."

"—and in the process of changing it, you sometimes employ a form of thought. But this is not unity.

"You impose an illusion on yourselves, thinking that only matter has substance, that thought and energy are insubstantial. They are all the same thing; all are interchangeable."

"Mystical twaddle," Bones said.

"Not at all. You invent 'laws' of nature that supposedly provide a description of the physical universe.

71

Actually, they only describe your isolation from reality.

"You build machines in accordance with these 'laws,' and try to use them to cope with the universe —but all this does is move you farther away from arivne."

Kirk: "And that's why our machines stopped working?"

"We limited your use of them to an absolute minimum, necessary for your survival. Even this is too much for our comfort. It is like trying to live in the midst of a loud, unpleasant noise, constantly varying."

"You don't seem all that concerned about our safety," Bones pointed out. "One man dead because the phasers don't work; another killed by your own actions."

"That was unfortunate. In the first case, we had overestimated your muscular strength. In the second, the ones who attacked you were immature, just made. They were still in the tool-using phase of their growing, and had more curiosity than moral sense. Again, we were surprised they could harm you."

"Then you're admitting that your judgment, your intelligence, isn't perfect," Bones said. "Who are 'you,' anyhow? What name does your race go by?"

"There is no sound that corresponds to our name. You may call us by the Vulcan term: the Arivne.

"No, our intelligence is not perfect. And it's less efficient than usual, with the 'noise' you and your machines make—in fact, your own brains are as up-setting as machines. Clatter, clatter. We'll have to be rid of some of you."

"Get rid of us?" Bones clenched his fists. "That doesn't say much for your own moral sense—or will you have the children do it?"

"The immature ones, like myself, would be un-

able. But it is not a moral problem, only a practical one. It will require more help than building this roof.

"And I do need sleep, to continue growing my body. This may not be the time—there."

All of the shuttles and most of the people disappeared. Only Spock, McCoy, Follett, Atheling, Charvat, and Ybarra were left.

"All of us scientists," Spock observed. "Why is that?"

"It was desired."

McCoy jumped at Hixon. "Murderer!" He bounced off something invisible and soft.

"I must sleep." Hixon lay down where he was standing. McCoy tried to approach him, but the barrier was still there.

"At least we have food," Charvat said. "They must be planning to keep us alive for a while." It looked like all of the food and medical supplies had been left behind.

"One wonders why, if he was telling the truth," Atheling said. "At any rate, it would probably be wise for us to take advantage of his sleeping, if anyone has something to say that he doesn't want overheard." They sat down to breakfast and quiet talk.

11

Ensign Bill Johnson, despite his very human-sounding name, was one of the eight *Enterprise* crewmen classified as aliens. His paternal grandfather was a Tarl from Epsilon Indi: this heritage gave him greenish skin, unusual height, high intelligence, and a metabolism that required large amounts of alcohol and total abstinence from acids, at least while on duty.

Every four hours he consumed a liter of 190-proof brandy. He'd just finished his second liter of the day, and what he saw made him suspect it had been spiked with orange juice.

The shuttles they had left behind on Anomaly were back in their bays.

There were twelve people on the hangar deck; one of them was Captain Kirk.

He unfolded his two-and-a-half meters from underneath the shuttle he was servicing and scrambled down a ladder to meet them.

"Ensign Johnson, sir. Can I help you?"

"Um, probably not, Ensign. Carry on." A few seconds ago, they'd been standing in the stockade. Then everything dissolved in a shower of sparks, and here they were. They walked toward the turbolift like people in a trance.

When Kirk and Uhura stepped out of the lift

onto the bridge, Scotty went through four distinct moods in less than thirty seconds:

He looked like he'd seen ghosts.

He was elated that they were safe.

He was worried about Spock, McCoy, and the others.

He was relieved to step down from the CO's chair.

Kirk gave them a brief outline of what had happened, and scheduled a general meeting and mutual debriefing for that evening.

"Have you made contact with Star Fleet Command?" he asked Czyzak, Uhura's stand-in.

"No, sir," she said, "though we've been sending out an automatic distress signal every fifteen minutes. Whatever interference these ... Arivne imposed, it's still as strong as it ever was."

"Well, sooner or later Academy is going to wonder why we haven't tried to contact them; that may start something.

"I don't like this feeling that we're running away from trouble, no more than anyone else. But it still seems the most reasonable course of action. If we were to turn about and attempt to rescue the seven who are still there ... no telling what the Arivne would do. We'd be risking the *Enterprise* and all hands." Kirk was really talking to himself, of course; trying to justify retreat from an enemy who held his two best friends prisoner.

"Sir," Czyzak said, "it's possible that help *is* on its way. Even though we haven't received any message from Star Fleet Command, our distress signal might be getting through. There's no way to test it, without coming to a dead stop and sending out a probe."

"But that would take days, wouldn't it?"

"At least a week, sir. For the probe to get far enough away to test subspace."

75

"Well, we can't afford it . . . what is the distress signal? How much information?"

"More than enough to make our situation clear, sir. We compressed ten minutes of transmission into a three-second bleat. It has a general description of what happened, along with various supporting documents —excerpts from the ship's log, biosensor readings, and so forth."

"Very good, Ensign. I suppose we can add to it now, though. Would you mind running it?"

"Right away, sir."

They were in for a surprise.

DISTRESS DISTRESS DISTRESS DISTRESS

This is Captain James T. Kirk, commander of the heavy cruiser *Enterprise,* currently en route to Academy. This recording is being made on Stardate 6136.6; date and time of transmission are COMPUTER INSERT. Our current position is COMPUTER INSERT.

A disaster has befallen the *Enterprise.* I believe myself to be unaffected by it so far, but have no reason to believe my immunity will continue. Therefore I am putting this recording into "permanent transmission" mode; neither I nor anybody else aboard the *Enterprise* can alter or end it.

Our trouble began when we stopped at the research station on Nesta, to pick up Professor James Atheling. Our normal duties were to be suspended for four weeks, in order to transfer Dr. Atheling to Academy, where he has been appointed dean of Star Fleet's College of Science.

Several science officers beamed down to the surface of Nesta, because they were interested in seeing Dr. Atheling's establishment there. Included were the three senior science officers, the chief surgeon, and one ensign, who had a professional interest in nonthermal sources of boson radiation.

All five, plus Dr. Atheling, were beamed up dead.

No immediate cause of death was found; but we discovered too late that the bodies were carriers of some disease with both physical and psychic symptoms.

The disease causes a protracted high fever, which has killed about 30% of the crew. Most of these were medical and transporter technicians.

Those who survive the fever (and other relatively minor physical symptoms) fall victim to a uniform, highly-detailed delusion. They all "remember" a fantastic series of incidents involving an Earth-sized rogue planet, inhabited by a race of superior telepathic humanoids.

Even if such a planet could exist, it seems unlikely that we would have stopped there without making any record of the fact. Here is the only log entry for that day:

Captain's Log, Stardate 6133.4:

This is Captain James T. Kirk, Commander.

The bodies of Spock, McCoy, Charvat, Follett, Ybarra, and Dr. Atheling have been placed in the biological stasis chamber, for more thorough analysis on Academy. The consensus of opinion is that some manner of transporter accident killed them. Accordingly, we will not use the transporters until they can be tested under laboratory conditions.

Lieutenant Commander Scott and several other people in Engineering are very ill with a fever. Nurse Chapel has recommended a quarantine of the section, if many more people come down with it.

> **Morale in general seems very low. Both Spock and McCoy were well-liked by the crew.**

> Those who've fallen prey to the delusion believe that the ones who died on Nesta (or between Nesta and the *Enterprise*) are still alive, and being held prisoner on the rogue planet. Please ignore any transmissions relating this story, even if they come from me.
>
> Further evidence, in the form of log entries and interviews with crewmen (those with the delusion and without), is here appended.

"Good God in heaven," Scott said, his brogue shocked completely away.

"I would bet any amount," Kirk said drily, "that the transmission is getting through."

"That's for sure," Uhura said slowly. "But, Captain . . . it does tell us one reassuring thing."

"Always in the market for good news."

"It shows us a limit of their powers. They can plant a fake story in the computer—but not in our heads! *I* still remember what happened, and so do you. Scotty? Did any of that happen, according to your memory?"

"No' a bit."

"Anybody?" Nobody on the bridge.

Kirk touched a button. "Computer."

"Working," it said.

"I would like to reprogram the distress message recorded on Stardate 6136.6: please erase."

"Won't work," Uhura muttered.

"This is contrary to my initial instructions."

"What difference does that make? This is Caprecorded on Stardate 6136.6: please erase."

"Captain, when you recorded the original message you specifically instructed me to ignore any subsequent changes, by you or any other crew member."

Kirk reddened. "Are you aware that I was not even aboard the *Enterprise* on Stardate 6136.6?"

"If you were not aboard, you could not have recorded the message, Captain. I detect human error."

"Endit! Uhura! Can you get at that message physically? Tear out the wiring?"

"I wouldn't advise it, sir. It would—"

"Can you?"

"Yes, sir."

Kirk realized he had risen half out of his chair, and sat back down. "I'm sorry, Lieutenant. What would it do?"

"Sir, it would disable the entire system."

"No way to get to just the message? Programming, rather than physically?"

"I don't think so, sir. The Arivne fixed it so that there's an unbreakable loop."

"Uh, Captain," Sulu said, "I almost hate to bring this up . . . but there's another possibility. The computer could be right."

They all stared at him. "If we did have the disease it describes, this is exactly the way we'd be acting."

Kirk laughed. "You're right, you know? Shouldn't be hard to check, though."

A quick check showed that the crewmen supposedly dead of the fever were still alive. The shuttles they'd gone to Anomaly with showed evidence of the trip (Johnson complained about the burn streaks on Shuttle #1, caused by the brush fire). But everything in the computer's memory was consistent with its own story.

They moved the briefing to the recreation area on Deck 20, so there would be room for all off-duty personnel. Over two hundred showed up.

Kirk and Uhura spent a half-hour telling what had

happened on Anomaly, and how the Arivne had subverted the ship's computer.

"I'm glad so many of you could come," Kirk said. "I have a difficult decision to make, and would value various opinions; a consensus." Star Fleet was not a democracy, of course, but there were some situations where the commander might be influenced by the commanded.

"It's not difficult to predict what will happen when we dock at Academy, this fabricated distress signal having preceded us. We'll be quarantined. And nothing we tell them about Anomaly will be of interest to them—except clinically—until they're convinced of the truth.

"How long the quarantine will last ... depends. If they beam someone aboard, we can show physical proof, and perhaps be free within a few hours.

"I think it's more likely to be days. Weeks, if they decide to call in specialists from other worlds. If the 'plague' were simply physical, transmitted by some organism, they would beam someone aboard in a protective suit, and that would be the end of it. Since it supposedly has psychic aspects, though, they're likely to be extremely cautious.

"I don't think we can afford the time. I think we ought to take a chance, and go back." Murmurs.

"Belay that, please ... hear me out. I won't pretend there's no element of risk; we have only the vaguest idea of the limits to the Arivne's powers. But we do have reason to believe that they have respect for life, and that they can't influence your mind, other than talking to you telepathically."

"Sir?" A hand went up.

"Ensign Sikh?"

"Begging your pardon, sir, that seems to me a false assumption. That Security lieutenant—"

"Hixon," someone supplied.

"—Lieutenant Hixon, they evidently compelled him to walk into the jungle at night, and submit to extreme mutilation, even though it was presumably painless. Hixon claimed to be happier that way, but I don't think I would be." There was a grumble of assent.

"I'm glad you brought that up," Kirk said, though he wasn't. "I talked with Mr. Spock and Dr. McCoy about that, last night. Mr. Hixon was under the influence of a very strong hypnotic. If you could get his attention, you could probably get him to do anything.

"Also, he wasn't ... mutilated by surgery. The evidence is that he did it with his own mind, since by the next morning he had continued the process on his own, without leaving the shuttle.

"The most compelling argument, though, is that they *only* did it to Hixon. It seems logical that they would have changed all of us, if that were in their power."

Uhura nodded. "Our alien way of thinking made them uncomfortable. 'Clatter, clatter,' Hixon said."

"Sir," Chekov said, "there's another possibility that shouldn't be ignored. Suppose they *could* alter people's minds, memories. The twelve of you who came back could be bait for the rest of us, to talk us into taking the *Enterprise* back to Anomaly."

"That wouldn't be very logical," Nurse Chapel said. "For one thing, Captain Kirk could simply turn the ship around, without having to explain his reasons to anybody. For another, they *had* the *Enterprise* for two days, if they'd wanted it. And if they could do anything with it, besides meddling with the computer."

"Captain." Lieutenant Commander Borido, chief of Security, stood up. "I know I speak for all of my people: we must go back. We can't abandon those six men and women to Hixon's fate. And we can't ignore the fact that they allowed two of our men to die, when it was within their power to prevent it."

"Thank you, Mr. Borido." Kirk tried to choose his words carefully. "You raise an interesting point. I think it would be a mistake for us to return in a spirit of revenge . . . as you point out, the only harm they have done to us has been out of carelessness and, well, misunderstanding of human nature.

"Our going back to Anomaly has to be a show of concern, not a show of force. Their intelligence is alien, but evidently acute. Perhaps we can make them understand."

Kirk could tell that most of the people in the lounge wanted to try it. "*Time* is the critical factor. Even if we only spend a day or two on Academy, it will be five weeks before we can get back. Even at that, we can't go straight to Anomaly, since we have no record of its position. By inference, we can narrow it down to a volume of about half a cubic light year—but an Earth-sized planet is a mighty small speck; we may have to search for weeks more!

"I don't want to gloss over the risks involved; I wish there were some way to make this a volunteer mission, but there isn't." He paused. "I've stated my case. Anybody else who wants the floor can have it."

Sharing a room with two hundred people all talking at once could make you sympathize with the Arivne. After a few minutes, things started to quiet down. The assistant chief engineer's strong contralto rang out:

"Captain, I've spoken to most of our people, and I already know Mr. Scott's opinion. Engineering is for the idea."

"And Medical," Nurse Chapel said.

"Communications."

"Ordnance."

"Sciences."

"Navigation."

Kirk nodded, and allowed himself to smile. "Mr. Scott," he said into the air.

"Aye, Captain," the wall speaker answered.

"Execute Plan A, if you please: Warp Factor Six."

"Aye, sir."

12

"It's possible they didn't destroy the others," Follett said. "They might have just sent them away..."

"Away to where?" Atheling said.

"I don't know, a cave or something. Who knows where you would put people, to insulate yourself from their thoughts?"

"There can't be any place on this planet," Bones said, "that wouldn't be a death sentence, unprotected. Besides, he said 'be rid of you.' I think that's pretty clear."

Charvat finished his meal and rolled the container into a tight ball. "And when they're through with us, we'll get the same treatment. Or wind up like poor Hixon."

Spock wasn't eating. Few of the meals they'd left behind were meatless; he was saving them. "This is an unproductive line of speculation. Whatever happens, it's unlikely we'll have any control over it."

"That's true," Atheling said. "What's more interesting is why did they spare six of us, and why this particular six? If our presence bothers them so much, why didn't they save just one...or two—a human and a Vulcan."

"Dr. Atheling, you're working under what could be a false assumption," Ybarra said. "That they spared the six of us to study us. Maybe five humans and a Vulcan is what they need to make a meat loaf."

There was an uncomfortable silence. "He said they don't eat," Follett said.

"Maybe they feed the animals." Charvat threw the balled-up foil at Hixon. It bounced off something invisible.

With a faint *pop,* an Arivne appeared next to them. It was slightly larger than the one they'd captured, and its hair was long and silky, red mixed with white. It "looked" at them and all five humans winced with a sudden blinding headache. It turned away quickly and the headaches were gone.

"Very interesting," Spock said.

Bones was kneading his temples. "What? You could understand that?"

"Only a little, through the pain. In a way, it apologized. It's going to wake up Hixon and talk to us through him."

Hixon stirred and sat up. The hair on his body was noticeably longer. He yawned—a shock; his tongue was gone—and faced the Arivne.

The new one's "voice" was different. It made a cold feeling in the brain. *"I have been nearby, and was listening to your discussion through this one as he slept.*

"I want to reassure you. Your friends should be safe. With considerable effort, we sent them back to your vessel. It is extremely far away and moving very fast, so we can't be perfectly sure. However, this one described to us the room with the largest volume inside the vessel, which gave us a place to aim for with reasonable confidence."

"Suppose you missed, though," Charvat said. "What happened to the people?"

"They are somewhere near the vessel. Within a few thousand of your kilometers. Almost certainly dead."

"You can send them there but you can't tell whether they made it," McCoy said.

"True. This is because the vessel is receding from us. If it were approaching us, or stationary, we could contact them the way we are speaking to you."

"You could reassure us even further," Atheling said, "if you would tell us why we're being held here. And why us, rather than some other—"

"You are being held here for study. Not food, as one of you suggested."

"Why us?" Atheling repeated.

"That is not important to you."

"Why would you want to study us in the first place?" Spock asked.

"That is of no importance to you, either." He disappeared with the same small noise. Hixon slumped back to sleep.

"That was a funny question, Spock," Charvat said.

"Not at all. Could you perceive anything of its personality?"

"Personality? Not much. Coldness ... reserve ... superiority. Mostly just words, though."

"Perhaps my experience with mind-melding makes me more sensitive to this—"

"That's logical," McCoy said, with a straight face.

"Indeed. What you see as 'superiority' I feel is only one facet of an overwhelming sense of confidence. Confidence in its ability to deal with any problem, physical or intellectual—though it would claim there is no difference between the two.

"The reason I asked the question was that I could see absolutely no element of curiosity in its personality. None. It has such unshakable faith in its interpretation of reality that it . . . feels no need to enquire further.

"I can't imagine why it would want to study us. It seems to have no psychological need to learn."

"It's obviously hiding something," Charvat said.

"I wonder," Spock said. "That implies there is some way we could harm them."

"Say, Spock," McCoy drawled, "why don't you just—"

"Don't say it, Dr. McCoy. I don't think they can read our minds unless we focus our thoughts by speaking."

"You know what I was going to say, though."

"Yes. It is worth trying, when the opportunity presents itself. Right now we should talk of anything else . . . did you know that the Arivne concept of the interdependence of thought, matter, and energy has a counterpart in human physics?"

"Do tell." Bones pretended to stifle a yawn.

"Yes. It begins back in the twentieth century, with Schrödinger's Cat, a paradox introduced to demonstrate a flaw in the application of conventional ideas of causality to quantum-mechanical situations. . . ."

The idea that had occurred to both McCoy and Spock was for Spock to mind-meld with Hixon; eavesdropping on the Arivne for a few moments. Spock couldn't have been looking forward to it. Mind-melding was physically painful and psychologically disturbing; to do it Spock had to shed all of his Vulcan reserve and make a kind of emotional contact with the subject.

McCoy didn't have to pretend being bored any longer, after two solid hours of listening to the others drone on and on about ontology and quantum mechanics. He'd had to suffer through two semesters of physics in medical school, and had mercifully forgotten all of it.

Hixon sat up, stood, and faced them. The transformation was continuing: his arms and legs seemed to

87

be longer; he had absorbed his large toes and genitalia; the hair was almost two centimeters long.

"Now. We can begin." He walked toward them. *"There are tests—"* As he walked by Spock, the Vulcan stood up quickly and clamped both hands on his head.

Spock let out an unearthly scream and collapsed.

"That was not smart." He gestured to McCoy. *"You, Doctor, see whether he has killed himself."*

McCoy knelt by Spock and felt the lower right part of his chest. "He has a heartbeat. Not as fast as it should be . . . I'll let him rest for a while, not try anything fancy."

"All right. He must never do that again. We have nothing to hide from you; nothing that concerns you.

"Even my mind is too powerful for him to attempt direct communication. If he had tried that with any adult, it would certainly have killed him."

"You said something about tests?" Charvat said.

"Yes. It would be convenient if we could have your cooperation for this.

"We wish to send you back to your own pasts, and relive with you the way you solved, or failed to solve, a problem."

"What does our cooperation have to do with it?" McCoy said, keeping his hand on Spock's chest. "If you're so—"

"It would be very painful to you, and probably destructive, for us to probe that deeply, and without speech as a focusing aid. What we require is for Dr. McCoy to administer hypnotics, in similar dosage to what he gave me—"

"And have us all wind up like you? You're out of your mind!"

"There is no chance of that. We needed one hu-man as a communication liaison. To change more than one would only be added work and discomfort.

"Besides, you are at our mercy. If we were to lose interest in you, it's unlikely that you could survive."

Bones was the wrong man to threaten. "Why don't we just wait a little while . . . find out whether Mr. Spock learned anything of interest."

As if on cue, Spock sighed and sat halfway up; rolled over onto his side. "They . . . need us. They—"

"Stop! This may interfere with the test."

"What test?" Spock asked.

Hixon explained briefly.

"You may be correct," Spock said. "I'm willing to wait.

"You mean you think we should go through with it?" McCoy said. "Let them be in total control?"

"Don't worry about this! We would not change another human even if you desired it, as you should."

"From what I saw," Spock said, "he's telling the truth. This 'test,' this regression, may not be particularly pleasant, but they won't tamper with anything but our memories."

"All right." McCoy went to the supply pile and brought back the bottle of pills and some water. "Who's first?" he asked Hixon.

"Mr. Spock will be first."

Bones scratched his chin. "Is this gonna work? I don't even know how much to give you."

"The usual human dosage should be sufficient. I have a certain amount of control over my metabolism, as you know."

He tried to think of something sarcastic to say. "Sure." Spock took the pills, leaned back, and closed his eyes.

SPOCK*

It was a relief to be away from the cool, damp air and light gravity of the *Enterprise,* to be back on Vulcan. But that pleasure only registered in one small corner of Spock's mind: he was in the grip of *pon farr,* the time of mating.

He stood with Kirk and McCoy at *Koon-ut-Kal-if-fee,* "the place of marriage and challenge." His family had used it for a hundred generations—long enough for windblown rain and scouring sand to soften the edges of the great stone blocks that defined the circular arena. Some had shifted from their upright position, or even tumbled over, but tradition forbade repair. The chiseled inscriptions on the rocks had faded to illegible dimples.

The sky was a blue so pale it was nearly white; the brilliant sun almost overhead. A hot, neverceasing wind blew stinging sand.

In the center of the circle, two stone arches made a rough temple over an open fire pit. Large slabs of green crystal hung together, ponderous bass chimes turning in the wind.

Kirk had spoken of Terran animals—salmon, eels —who travel great distances to arrive at a certain place for mating. He could never understand. This was nothing so simple as sexual tension. Neither was it cerebral, like a formal ritual, though to outward appearance much of it would seem to be.

The *pon farr* transcended body and brain; it was a bond of *kah,* for which no human word could exist. To deny it, to always be somewhere else when *pon farr*

---

*The action in this scene is taken from "Amok Time" in *Star Trek 3* (Bantam, 1969), adapted by James Blish from the original *Star Trek* script by Theodore Sturgeon.

came upon you, eventually meant death—and death was only the least of what it was.

At the age of seven, Spock had been bound to T'Pring, his future mate, in a process similar to mind-melding. Although hundreds of light-years had separated them for most of their lives, the *kah* remained, unattenuated by space or time. It was a passive link, unnoticed by either, until *pon farr* approached. Spock resisted a few cycles, but finally it would not be denied: Spock was drawn to *Koon-ut-Kal-if-fee* as a dropped stone is drawn to earth.

Traditionally, a Vulcan male brought his two closest friends to stand *pon farr* with him. Their historic function was similar to that of seconds in a duel—because in ancient days, when Vulcans had been less gentle and rational, males fought for their mates, fought to the death. This would happen whenever the female declared *kah-if-farr*, a rejection of her parents' choice. She would name her own choice of a mate; the one who left the arena alive would be her husband.

The forms were retained—even to the use of ancient weapons in the ceremony—but blood was rarely spilled. The couple would go ahead with the ceremony even if one or both of them desired a different mate. Once the ceremony was over, and the *kah* dissolved, they would go to a council of elders, who would reluctantly grant an annulment. It was not as bad as *kah-if-farr* (which was technically legal, and still happened on occasion), but it was a terrible breach of tradition, with permanent social consequences.

Spock had had no close Vulcan friends since leaving the planet for Academy, so he chose Kirk and McCoy to stand with him. The probability that they would have to fight was vanishingly small—a good thing, since they would be handicapped by the higher gravity and their unfamiliarity with the antique weapons.

Barely audible, then growing stronger, a musical tinkling overlay the booming sound of the chimes. A small procession of Vulcans approached the arena. One, borne on a litter, was an old woman named T'Pau, one of the most powerful figures in Vulcan politics; even Kirk recognized her. Beside her walked Spock's bride, T'Pring, beautiful by the standards of either Vulcan or Earth. Two male Vulcans followed her; the second a short, muscular man carrying a Vulcan war axe. Two others carried ceremonial frames hung with dozens of tiny bells. The rest of the procession walked slowly behind them.

The men carrying the litter lowered it, and T'Pau stepped from it with easy grace. Spock left the two humans and walked up to one of the large jade chimes. He struck it with a stone mallet, and the deep boom was answered with a shaking of the ceremonial frames. T'Pring sat on a carved rock at the temple archway; T'Pau stood with her back to her, in front of the temple.

T'Pau thrust both arms into the air. Spock bowed before her; she placed hands on his shoulders in benediction. She stared at the two humans.

"Spock. Are our ceremonies for outworlders?"

"They are not outworlders; they are my friends," Spock said. "I am permitted this. Their names are Kirk and McCoy. I pledge their behavior with my life."

"Very well." She turned to the entourage, gathered in a line facing the temple, and said the word that would start the ceremony: *"Kah-if-fee!"*

The small bells answered her. Spock turned to sound the wind chimes again—but suddenly his bride T'Pring jumped up and shouted "Kah-if-*FARR!*"

The challenge.

The onlookers gasped with surprise—not a common thing among Vulcans—and Spock's lips moved, repeating the word silently. A change came over him.

Panting, Spock watched T'Pring with slitted eyes. She walked toward him with a contemptuous half-smile, took the stone mallet from his grip, and tossed it aside. She turned her back on him and moved into the arena.

The Vulcan with the axe stepped forward, testing its edge with his thumb.

"Hey, what's this?" McCoy said. "If there's going to be hanky-panky . . ."

"All is in order," T'Pau said. "She chooses the challenge."

"What?" McCoy pointed at the man with the axe. "With *him?*"

"No. He acts only if cowardice is seen. T'Pring will now choose her champion. T'Pring: you have chosen. Are you prepared to become the property of the victor? Not merely his wife, but his chattel, with no other rights or status?"

"I am prepared."

"Then choose."

The big young Vulcan who had followed T'Pring in the procession stood up straight, chest out, as she approached him. But she moved on by, and turned to face T'Pau.

"As it was in the dawn of our days," she said, "as it is today, as it will be through all tomorrows . . . I make my choice."

She pointed at Kirk. "I choose this man."

Kirk started to protest, but he was drowned out by the big young Vulcan. "No!" he cried, outraged. "I am to be the one! It was agreed! The honor is mine!"

Spock stood glowering, fists clenched, while the marriage party argued loudly in Vulcan. He paid no attention to them, nor to Kirk and McCoy, who were whispering together.

T'Pau stopped the noise with a single explosive word: *"Kroykah!"*

The Vulcan who had not been chosen, who had been arguing the loudest, stared at the ground and said, "I ask forgiveness." He returned to where he'd been standing, by the arch, and slouched there, not repentant.

T'Pau looked at Kirk questioningly.

"I accept." Spock showed no sign of hearing.

Two Vulcans stepped forward with the weapons: staves a little more than a meter long, with a blade on one end and a club on the other. The blades were half-moon-shaped, and looked keen as razors; the clubs were metal bludgeons almost the size of a man's head.

"According to our laws, combat begins with the *lirpa,*" T'Pau said, naming the weapon. "If both survive the *lirpa,* then combat continues with *ahn woon,* until death." The Vulcan men handed the weapons to the two combatants. *"Klee-et!"*

Spock whirled around to face Kirk, eyes blazing.

McCoy stepped forward. "Nothing doing! No one mentioned a fight to the death . . ." The axe-wielding Vulcan moved toward him, lifting his weapon. McCoy continued, more calmly. "T'Pau, these men are friends. To force them to fight until one is killed . . ."

"Challenge was lawfully given and accepted. Neither party was forced. However, Spock may release the challenger. Spock! How do you choose?"

Spock's intelligence, his compassion, were completely blanked out by the white heat of *kah*. He glared at Kirk without recognizing him. *"Klee-fah!"* he shouted.

Kirk, eyes on Spock, told McCoy to get out of the

combat area. McCoy continued to protest—but suddenly, Spock lunged.

Kirk dodged the blade but the attack was a feint: Spock swung the cudgel end around and dealt Kirk a glancing blow. Kirk went down, rolling; Spock slashed at him but missed. While the Vulcan was off-balance, Kirk kicked at his legs and knocked him down, then staggered to his feet, already tiring in the heat and high gravity.

McCoy faced T'Pau, holding out a hypo from his medical kit. "Are Vulcans afraid of fair combat?" he asked.

"What is this?"

"A high-gee vitalizer shot. To compensate for temperature and atmosphere."

"Kroykah!" With that command, again, everyone froze. She paused, then told McCoy to go ahead; the request was reasonable.

Bones gave him the shot, and then—*Klee-et!*— the fighting resumed. They were evenly matched now, thrusting and parrying as though choreographed.

Suddenly the two men crashed together, each grabbing the other's weapon wrist, locked in a contest of brute strength.

Spock won. Kirk's *lirpa* spun to the ground, and Spock leaped to stamp on it, breaking the fragile blade. He kicked it away and advanced on his captain, blade raised for the kill.

"Spock!" McCoy yelled. "No!" The Vulcan made no sign of hearing him.

But Kirk surprised him—a feint, then a rapid karate chop, and Spock's own weapon whirled away.

"Kroykah!" T'Pau stopped the first phase of the contest. They had survived the *lirpa;* the *ahn woon* would determine the victor. A weapons attendant

brought them two meter-long leather strips, with handles.

Kirk looked at it, puzzled. "A strip of leather? Is that all?"

While T'Pau was explaining to him that the *ahn woon* was the oldest and deadliest of Vulcan weapons —having both short-range and long-range functions— Spock picked up a jagged rock and looped the strip into a sling, and flung the rock at Kirk's chest. It struck, and the crowd murmured surprise. A Vulcan would have dodged it.

Kirk fell, but staggered back to his feet. Spock moved in and whipped the *ahn woon* around his legs, bringing him down again.

That was it. Spock coiled the leather strap around Kirk's neck and pulled it tight, garroting him. Kirk plucked feebly at the weapon. His eyes bulged and his face turned scarlet. Then he went limp . . . dead.

"*Kroykah!*" The contest was over.

McCoy's voice was flat, bitter: "Get your hands off him, Spock. It's finished—he's dead."

That moment the *kah* broke. Spock was Spock again.

T'Pau and McCoy were talking, but Spock didn't hear. The one man in the universe he could call "friend" lay dead at his feet. Spock knew that he hadn't killed Kirk; *kah* had done it, with Spock a helpless intermediary. It didn't help.

"No!" Kirk dead? "I—no, no . . ."

Is it possible for a Vulcan to lose his sanity? For a few moments, the human side of him—plunged into suicidal grief—warred with the stoic Vulcan aspect: remorseless logic would absolve him of guilt; nevertheless, if he were not punished for this, who would be?

McCoy was talking into his communicator. ". . . stand by for landing party to beam up." He turned

96

to Spock. "Strange as it may seem, Mr. Spock, you're in command now. Any orders?"

"I'll—I'll follow you in a few minutes. Instruct Mr. Chekov to plot a course for the nearest base ... where I must surrender myself to the authorities."

McCoy gone, Spock asked T'Pring why she had forced him to fight and kill Captain Kirk. It was because she'd wanted Stonn, the big Vulcan who had been so outraged at not being chosen her champion. With Spock and Kirk fighting, she would be assured of having Stonn, no matter who won. Spock commended her on her logic.

To Stonn, he said, "After a time, you may find that *having* is not, after all, so satisfying a thing as *wanting*. It is not logical, but it is often true ..." He kept his self-control long enough to say goodbye to T'Pau, and be beamed up.

When he was finally alone, on the turbolift from the transporter room to sick bay, he began to weep uncontrollably.

He was back on Anomaly, lying on the ground, curled into a ball. He wiped tears off his cheeks and looked up at Hixon.

"Why did you choose that particular incident?" he asked. "Nothing could have been less characteristic." As he spoke, he remembered the rest of it: Kirk hadn't died; the "high-gee vitalizer" Dr. McCoy had given him was actually ronoxoline-D, which had put him in a coma so deep he had appeared to be dead.

"We are not interested in the Vulcan side of you. There is nothing you can teach us about logic. Quickly now, the next: Dr. McCoy."

McCoy and the others were on the other side of the circle, lashing together a sort of a lean-to, as a privacy barrier for the portable head that had been left with the other supplies (building it with the stakes Atheling had dutifully sharpened to put in the moat). They may have chosen this opportunity in order to spare themselves the inevitable argument about the logic of modesty in the present situation.

McCoy crossed over. "That took quite a while, Spock."

"How long?"

"Almost two hours." He looked closely at Spock. "Your face is dirty."

Spock rubbed at his cheek and nodded. "Real time, then. That's about how long the incident took."

"You will take the pills, Doctor."

He hesitated. "What should I expect, Spock?"

"I don't know. I suspect it will be psychologically painful. Emotionally painful."

"But you think it's worth it."

"Believe me, Doctor. From what I saw ... even death would be a reasonable proposition."

He swallowed the pills and sat down, waiting for them to take hold.

McCOY

McCoy let himself into the apartment and shouted hello to Honey and Joanna, who were back in the little girl's bedroom. He changed out of his hospital whites and mixed himself a strong bourbon-and-water. It had been a hard day, an ordinary day.

He went to the newspaper machine and punched up WORLD NEWS, EDITORIAL & FEATURE, and COMIX. The machine chuckled for a moment and disgorged about fifty sheets of paper.

Settled in his favorite chair, he finished the comics and most of the features before he noticed that Honey and Joanna were still in Joanna's room. Strange.

"Anything wrong in there?"

"We'll be out in a minute," Honey answered.

"What are you doing?" No answer.

Bones shrugged mentally and went on with his paper. After a few minutes, Honey and Joanna did come out, but not as far as the living room. They stopped in the hall, and Honey put down two of the three suitcases she was carrying, to palm the door open.

"Hey," McCoy said. "What are you doing?"

Honey faced him. "Leaving."

"What?"

"Good-bye, Leonard." Joanna looked terrified, holding her small suitcase against her body like a shield.

"Wait!" The papers scattered as McCoy levered himself out of the chair. "Just leaving? Just like that?"

"Now, Leonard——"

"Now, *hell!* You can't——"

"Joanna. Go back to your room and make sure there's nothing you missed."

"But Mommy," she squeaked, "we did that already."

"Go check one more time." She glared at McCoy as the little girl ran back down the hall.

"Now would you please explain——"

"You don't need any explanations. My lawyer will be in touch with you. Clear up the——"

"Is it too much trouble . . . to ask why?"

She walked two steps toward him and stopped, and said in a loud whisper: "I'm not happy. She's not happy. You're not happy. Do you want me to get more specific?"

"I always loved your sense of drama. No, I don't want you to be specific; I want you to be sensible. Stop acting like a——"

"When was the last time you made love to me?"

That stopped him for a second. "We've covered this territory before."

"March third. I marked it on the calendar."

"Now you listen—"

"That's over three weeks, Leonard. I'm not made of stone." She was crying. That made McCoy even madder—and then mad at himself.

"For Christ's sake, you know what the hospital's been like the past three weeks? Three *months?* You're lucky I even—"

"That's just the *point,* Leonard!" She dabbed at tears with a balled-up handkerchief. "We, we shouldn't've gotten married in the first place. There's no room in your life for a woman, for a wife and family . . . nothing but your precious emergency room and your fourteen-hour days. I can't make you feel important, so I'm not important to you."

"That's very good. Did you make that up yourself?"

"You're a cold, heartless man," she whispered. "Joanna!"

"We'll talk about this tomorrow, after you've had a chance to cool down."

"Oh, no, we won't." Joanna ran up and hid behind her mother.

"We do still have three years on our contract. Have you forgotten?"

"Tell it to the lawyer." She palmed the door and it slid open.

"Are you taking the flyer?"

"We're not taking anything of yours."

Except Joanna, McCoy thought. "Can I drop you somewhere?"

"No. Our ride's waiting. He'll take us to my sister's."

" 'He'? That's interesting."

"Nothing that would interest you." He watched them go down the steps, resisting an absurd impulse to help with the suitcases. The man in the flyer, a stranger, was staring at him. He palmed the door closed.

He wandered around the house for a while, feeling numb. He sat down at the prescription machine in his office and almost punched up a sleeping pill. He went into the kitchen and poured some straight whiskey into a glass, then poured it into the sink. He toyed with the idea of throwing the glass into the sink, to hear it break, but didn't.

In the living room, he picked up the scattered papers and stacked them neatly. An advertisement caught his eye:

SPACE FOR A FEW

A representative of Star Fleet Command, United Federation of Planets, will be interviewing prospective applicants for Star Fleet commissions tomorrow, from 9:00 AM to 5:00 PM, at the Jackson Mall. Openings exist for trained personnel in the following specialties:

Alien anthropology	Medicine (M.D. only)
Astronomy	Promorphology
Biology (esp. xenobiology)	Recreation
	Tachyon engineering
Catastrophics	Transporter technology
Chemical Engineering	Weapons systems
Discretion theory	Xenolinguistics
Environmental systems	

Unmarried people under the age of 40 may apply. Initial rank commensurate with training and experience.

Unmarried, McCoy thought, that's an interesting word. Can be either an adjective or a verb. Honey is going to unmarry me.

He put the stack of paper in the tray on top of the newspaper machine and pressed the RECYCLE button. It sucked the paper into a slot and growled for a few seconds.

His shift didn't start until 11:00 tomorrow. Jackson Mall. That would show the bitch.

Spock helped him up. "That didn't take very long."

"No." McCoy was groggy with the drug. "Glad. Strong stuff . . . you want to—"

"Sharon Follett."

"You want to tell me what this is all about now?" he asked Spock.

"After you administer the drug."

McCoy gave her the pills and watched her fall asleep. Moved away. "So. You said it might be worth dying for?"

"Yes. It could be that the fate of all races in the Federation is in the balance.

"There is an . . . association of races in the Sagittarius Arm, which he calls the Irapina. Like the Arivne, they are telepathic; unlike them, they are emotional and belligerent."

"Sagittarius Arm is pretty far away."

"True. But they are coming in this direction. They have been for a thousand years. They intend to conquer or destroy everything in their path, and so far they have an enviable record of success."

"And they're almost here?"

"No. Their main forces won't arrive for another thousand years. But they are in telepathic contact with the Arivne, and are in the process of deciding whether it would be worth sending an advance party ahead, to test them out. It's very expensive in terms of energy, sending scouts ahead; essentially, it would delay their invasion by more than a hundred years."

"What, are they immortal?"

"To all practical purposes. Immortal, but caught in adolescence, emotionally. Very dangerous."

"Good God. I wish Jim was here."

"*You may find your wish fulfilled, soon. They have turned the Enterprise around, and are returning.*"

13

Sharon Follett was forced to relive the sad and painful time when she had to choose between having a baby and staying in Star Fleet. She had an abortion.

Andre Charvat went back to Academy days, to a morning when he woke up to find that his roommate had committed suicide. Charvat, as had been required by law and custom, had reported the lad for cheating, the day before.

Rosaly Ybarra relived the most terrible hour of her life. Ten years old, she had decided not to go on a picnic. Her parents tired of cajoling her; packed up the rest of the family and left. She watched the flyer as it rose to about a hundred meters' altitude, then inexplicably tumbled to the ground, crashed, and burst into flame. It was fifteen years before she stopped blaming herself for her family's death.

When Hixon finished with Atheling, he promptly stretched out and went back to sleep.

Atheling was pale, trembling. Sharon Follett put an arm around his shoulder. "Pretty bad, Jim?"

"Yes. Um ... do I have to talk about it?" The others had.

"It could be useful," Spock said. "The Arivne don't seem anxious to elaborate on their plans. Any datum may help."

"Well, as with all of us . . . it involved guilt. But there was nothing especially dramatic about it.

"When I was an undergraduate I worked in the mathematics department part-time; I had a scholarship, but it didn't cover all my living expenses. So I'd come in a few days a week and type, sweep up, whatever.

"I was carrying a wastepaper basket to the recycling room, toward the end of my second year . . . on the top of the paper was a handwritten first draft of the final exam for a course I was taking. Theory of differential equations. I wasn't doing very well in the course, so after struggling with my conscience for about a tenth of a second, I snatched up the sheet and stuffed it in my pocket.

"The exam was just a couple of hours away, but that was long enough for me to cram enough specific information into my brain to assure that I'd get a perfect paper. And I did.

"But mine was the *only* perfect paper, by a long shot. I was sure the professor and the class knew I'd cheated, but nothing ever came of it. Except that I spent the whole summer becoming an expert on the subject, to assuage my guilt and make sure nobody ever caught me in my ignorance."

He hunched his shoulders. "It's interesting that the Arivne picked that incident. Objectively, it's a pretty trivial thing. But I have, and had then, rather inflexible ideas about honor. That one piece of deception has nagged at me for forty years."

"It seems to have gotten all of us where it hurts the most," Charvat said.

"True." He looked at Spock. "Can I be let in on the secret now?" Spock told him about the threat of the Irapina.

"One wonders, though," Atheling said, "what these various tragedies of ours have to do with their handling the invaders. What are we showing them?"

"I think the key is not tragedy, but decision. In our sense of the word, an Arivne never has to decide anything. With any problem, there is only one best course of action; perceiving it is the same as implementing it.

"Yet they know that the Irapina are faced with a decision—whether to send an advance guard here, to test them—and it could be that they want to experience the decision-making process, at least second-hand."

Atheling nodded. "And to make the most of it, they searched our memories for the one that had affected each of us most strongly."

The red-furred Arivne appeared then, its back to them; Hixon woke up and said, *That is essentially correct, as far as it goes.*

"We will repeat the process soon, to a different end. Before that, though, it has been decided that you should know more about the problem. Since your thought processes are similar to those of the Irapina, your reactions may provide us with new information.

"They are a formidable enemy. This is how they would appear to you."

An opaque cloud of vapor coalesced in front of them, and gradually took on solid form.

Bones summed it up: "Ugly son-of-a-bitch." He was putting it mildly.

It was something like a cross between a huge insect and a centaur. It stood on four massive legs, intricately jointed, covered with shiny black chitin. Its egg-shaped body was shiny brown, mottled with green and blue. A thorax rose from the front, covered with black bristles, supporting two arms and a head. The arms were strangely articulated, mechanical-looking things, that ended in clusters of writhing tentacles, rather than hands. One arm was twice the size of the other, and had a hooked claw at each of four elbows. The head was triangular, with eyes that looked like two clusters of pale red salmon eggs. The mouth was a small hole, through which a slender black tongue occasionally darted. It was about the size of a large horse. A thick barbed tail, like that of a scorpion, curved under its body.

"It's immortal?" Atheling asked.

"Not really; in that respect Mr. Spock was mistaken. They do live a long time by your standards—as much as two thousand years—but they do so by constantly replacing organs before they can fail.

"The largest class in their society is made up of individuals who are slaughtered as soon as they reach maturity; harvested for their organs. The Irapina are very clever surgeons."

"How many of them are there?" Charvat asked.

"In the expedition coming toward us, there are about ten billion. Perhaps one-quarter are adults of the . . . warrior/thinker/surgeon class. They are about 25,000 light years away."

"They could be here in a little more than a hundred years," Spock said, "at Warp Factor Six."

"True, but they aren't moving that fast. Their four vessels are almost the size of this planet.

"However, they can send individuals this distance instantaneously, at great expense of energy/thought. They have detected two races they may wish to visit, ourselves and the Organians.* They are in the process of deciding whether it will be necessary. It would delay their conquest."

---

*The Organians are beings of pure energy, inhabiting a planet in a region that lies between the Klingon Empire and Federation territory. They forced the two cultures to sign a peace treaty in the story "Errand of Mercy" (by Gene L. Coon; adapted by James Blish in *Star Trek 2;* Bantam, 1968), and also figured in the novel *Spock Must Die!* (by James Blish; Bantam, 1970).

"How soon will they decide?" McCoy asked.

"I don't know; this is why we sought more information about decision-making. They first contacted me about 40 years ago. I assume they have been 'deciding' ever since. Your presence here, though, is a complication. It may force them to decide, one way or the other, soon."

"That's strange," Charvat said. "It doesn't look like we're in any position to harm them."

"Now, you are not. But given a thousand years' warning, your Federation could become a dangerous obstacle to them. They may wish to kill all of you on this planet, in order to keep the invasion a secret."

"But they couldn't kill all of *you*."

"Not with one or two individuals. But the eventual ten billion could do so with ease. They have indicated that they may wish to offer me survival for my silence."

"And you'd do it?" McCoy said.

"It is my present course of action. You must try to understand: I bear you no ill will, and would rather have you exist as you do now, than see you destroyed or enslaved.

"But I would be of little help to you in a battle with the Irapina. My powers are attenuated by distance; I have little influence more than a light year or so from this planet.

"If a problem is of sufficient importance, all Arivne can work on it together; this is how we are able to communicate with the Irapina at such a vast distance. But even together, we couldn't so much as move a pebble on Earth or Vulcan."

"I thought matter, energy, and thought were all the same thing," Ybarra said.

"It is a matter of degree, rather than kind. In your own view of reality, consider the difference be-

tween a speck of dust and a planet made of the same material. They are manifestly equivalent—in chemistry, for instance—yet one you can manipulate with ease, and the other is beyond your powers."

"You mean to say you don't see any moral problem," McCoy said, "in abandoning the rest of us to fight this horde of monsters by ourselves?"

"Under the circumstances, no. Since no course of action would change the outcome for you, we act to preserve ourselves."

"But there is a flaw in your logic," Spock said. "You assume that you are bound to this planet. Star Fleet could distribute Arivne all around the Federation—"

"Absolutely not! We could never survive, being surrounded by your minds and machines."

The telepathic "voice" changed; it was Hixon: *"I have a suggestion. Given a thousand years, you could change a hundred thousand humans, or more, into half-Arivne, like myself. They could tolerate the presence of humans . . ."*

"It's possible. If not too many humans were on the planet at once—"

"Never work," McCoy said. "I doubt you'd find a hundred volunteers in the whole Federation. *I'd* never do it—rather fight and die a human."

"You are probably correct, though the position is not reasonable.

"Rest now. I'll return shortly." It disappeared. The image of the Irapina faded slowly.

Hixon went instantly back to sleep; the six humans sat in stunned silence.

"There's one thing we ought to consider," McCoy said. "It could be lying to us. To shock us into cooperation, or maybe just to observe our reactions."

"That's not impossible," Spock said, "but nothing

109

it told us was inconsistent with the impressions I got in mind-melding. Of course, those impressions would be accessible to it; if it were lying it shouldn't be difficult to stay consistent."

"Besides," Ybarra said, "that creature it showed us seemed so unlikely. Like a made-up nightmare."

Follett shook her head. "That doesn't mean anything. I've seen stranger animals . . . from a xenobiological viewpoint, the Arivne are stranger than this Irapina."

"And in the long run," Spock said, "possibly as dangerous."

14

Chekov looked up at the captain. "We're here," he said simply. They had arrived at the volume of space that they knew contained Anomaly, somewhere: a needle in a hay field.

"Sensors to maximum," Kirk said mechanically. "We'll begin quartering. Commence Lissajous course." They might find them immediately; it might take as long as two months.

Once the course was established, Kirk stood up. "Mr. Sulu, please take the bridge. I—"

"*Lysander* to *Enterprise.*" The face of an angry black man appeared on the main screen. "Respond!"

Kirk sat down and punched a button. "This is the *Enterprise.* Go ahead."

The man didn't seem to hear. He turned away from the screen. "Mr. Delacroix. Prepare to fire a torpedo over their bow." He turned back to face them. "*Lysander* to *Enterprise.* If you continue this evasive maneuvering, I shall be forced to take action."

"Captain!" Uhura said. "They're on EM, not subspace!" Her fingers stabbed at the buttons on the emergency override panel. "Use channel B."

"*Lysander* to *Enterprise!*" He was shouting.

"This is the *Enterprise.* Captain James Kirk, commanding."

111

He held up a hand and looked to his left. "Belay that. I am Captain Mohammed Tafari, commanding the destroyer *Lysander*. Please explain why you haven't responded to us before."

"Our subspace radio is out of order, Captain. How long have you—"

"We received your distress signal clearly enough. If this is some kind of a trap . . ."

"We can send, but not receive."

"I'm sorry, Mr. Kirk. My communications officer has assured me that that is not possible. It could only happen if your bridge intercom wasn't working. It obviously is."

"That would be true, sir," Uhura said, "under normal conditions."

"We've been sabotaged, Mr. Tafari. Our computer subverted—programmed with a false message that we can't override. There is no plague: the people supposedly dead are still alive."

Tafari looked at him for a moment. "Show me your first officer, then; the Vulcan. And your chief surgeon; I'd like to talk to them. I have pictures of them."

"They . . . they aren't here. They're being held captive on the planet—"

"I understand." He shook his head. "Captain Kirk, I hereby place you and your entire crew under medical detention. Your commission is temporarily revoked; from this moment I am in command of the *Enterprise*."

"You have orders to this effect?"

"Yes, I do. They have been transmitted to your computer. The *Lysander* will tow the *Enterprise* to Academy, where a team of specialists will analyze and treat the Nesta plague.

"I must warn you that anyone who attempts to beam aboard the *Lysander* will be destroyed on sight."

"And I assume that none of you will beam aboard the *Enterprise,* to verify my—"

"That is correct. My orders preclude any physical contact. Also, I am to minimize communications with you, on the chance that the psychic aspect of the disease could be transmitted that way.

"So I order you to shut down your engines. We will approach for tractor contact."

Kirk was somewhat nettled. "Not until I read the orders, Captain Tafari."

"Three minutes." The screen went black.

The orders did command that Kirk give up the *Enterprise* temporarily. He had no choice but to obey them—not only out of loyalty to the Federation, but out of practicality. The two ships were evenly matched in speed and armament, with the *Lysander* having an edge in maneuverability.

"Enterprise to *Lysander."*

Tafari's image appeared. "Well?"

"Everything seems to be in proper form. We will allow you to approach, but under the protest that . . ." Tafari cut off the communication in mid-sentence.

"Not very polite," Uhura said.

"He's probably not too enthusiastic about the mission," Kirk said. "Nursemaiding."

15

SPOCK

To ten-year-old Spock, Earth was physically uncomfortable but endlessly fascinating. His mother Amanda had brought him back to her own home planet, ostensibly to visit relatives, perhaps to leaven the austerity of his Vulcan upbringing.

Minneapolis/St. Paul/Hennepin was a vast urban complex, some 4,000 square kilometers of housing, parks, shopping areas, schools, and factories; nothing remotely like it existed on Vulcan. It was doubly strange because they were visiting in winter. Spock had never seen snow; in the parks and other places not domed over, the stuff lay around everywhere, blowing into drifts as tall as he was.

While Amanda visited her sister Doris, Spock tried to play with his cousins, Lester and Jimmy. He'd been discouraged from unstructured play for half his life, and had difficulty with the idea of "pretending." He was also, like all Vulcans, very sensitive to cold, and could only stay outdoors for short periods, even bundled up like a mummy.

Still, the child is father to the man: the curiosity about the physical universe that would be the adult Spock's main driving force was already very strong. For the first time in his life, Spock had a new planet to explore.

He might rather have done it alone. Lester and Jimmy were a year older and younger than he, respectively, and seemed immature and ignorant. He was as yet unskilled in hiding disdain, but was fortunately bigger and stronger than either of them. They retaliated when they could.

Spock was sitting on the floor of his aunt's library, reading *Hamlet*. He looked up when his mother came in, and removed his earmuffs.

"Son?"

"Yes, Mother?"

"There's been a little trouble. Come along with me."

In the living room, Doris stood with her children in front of the visiphone, which was ruined. The picture plate had been removed from the wall and opened; small electronic parts were scattered on the floor.

"Did you do this?" Amanda asked.

Spock looked at the two children. "No."

"You *did*, you *did!*" Lester said.

Jimmy was crying. "We was outside."

Doris chewed on her lower lip. "Amanda, I know you've said that Spock can't lie. But my children aren't physically strong enough to do this ... I've seen the repairman struggle with getting the picture plate open."

Amanda looked at her son, worried. "You don't have to be very strong," he said. "Not if you have two people and three screwdrivers. Lester and I did it yesterday—"

"Did *not!*"

"You have taken it apart, then?" Amanda said.

"Yes, to look inside. But I put it back together."

Now Lester was crying. "You gonna believe *him?*"

"Shush, now," she said gently, and gave

Amanda a pleading look. "But Spock is so . . . curious about everything . . ."

"Never untruthful. Obviously, he showed the boys—"

"*We didn't do it,*" Lester shrieked. "*I promise!*"

Jimmy echoed and elaborated: "Cross my heart, I promise!"

Doris covered her eyes with her hand. "Amanda, let's go into the kitchen and talk about this. You boys go back to what you were doing."

When the two adults had their backs turned, Jimmy and Lester stuck out their tongues at Spock, and pulled on their ears to make points. That evening, Spock and Amanda left.

McCOY

Although Leonard McCoy was on good terms with almost everybody aboard the *Enterprise,* he did like to get away by himself whenever shore leave presented the opportunity. And shore leave on Capory, a rather undeveloped planet circling Beta Hydri, was especially welcome. It was a wide-open frontier world, and Bones looked forward to letting his hair down.

He let his beard grow for a couple of days, and changed into shabby civilian clothes before he beamed down. In compliance with planetary law, he left his phaser behind, but carried along his communicator in case of trouble.

Capory's only important industry was pharmaceuticals. The planet was literally covered with mold. Prospectors would go out on flyer or foot to search for rare varieties hidden in the fetid jungles of moss and fungus. Animals also hid there, some with teeth and appetites, so the men and women went armed, and some never came back.

But the prizes were fabulous. A lucky find like Esio Telga (one dose of which would triple the life-span of a Stratosian) would make a person wealthy for life.

A tavern not far from the spaceport bore the predictable name *Last Chance/First Chance*. He stepped over a drunk and pushed his way through the swinging doors.

The interior was brightly lit and smoky. Most of the patrons were armed: flamers, spinpits, and line-shockers rather than the more potent phaser and ray gun. Deadly enough, though, for Bones to feel under-prepared.

The bartender was washing glasses under a sign that said CHECK YER WEAPONS. "Denebian brandy, please."

"Ne got." He didn't even look up. "Gi' ye corn er grape, in hard. Er beer."

"Uh, let me try a corn."

He wiped his hands on a greasy tunic and ladled half-a-liter of clear liquid into a glass mug. He set the mug on the bar but didn't let go of it. "Be se'en-five," he said.

"Seven-and-a-half credits?" Bones said doubtfully. He fingered the gold and silver coins in his pocket.

"Jess. Ye pays fer class."

Bones shook his head. "But I don't *want* the glass."

The bartender wheezed, laughing. A man sitting at the bar said, "*Class*, outworlder, not 'glass.' This is one of the best taverns in the city."

McCoy's mouth made a silent "oh" and he passed over a small gold coin, ten credits. The bartender bit it, looked at it, and let go of the mug. He banged a hand-ful of change down on the bar and turned his back.

Ten decims short; Bones decided not to make an issue of it.

Bones sat at an empty table and took a cautious sip. He expected raw alcohol, but to his relief it was rather mellow, if potent.

The man from the bar sat down across from him. "You're from Earth, aren't ye?"

"That's right."

"Me too. Haven't seen ye 'round."

"Haven't been around." McCoy wasn't sure whether he wanted company or solitude. "Just got in."

The man nodded. "Figgered it. Ye'd be off the *Solar Wind*?"

"Not supposed to say."

He stared at him for a moment, then laughed. "Understand. One thing sure, ye an't one of those boy heroes. That heavy cruiser up there."

Bones smiled. "Might be."

"Sure." He laughed again. "Me too. We won't tell anybody." He leaned forward confidentially. "Take a piece of advice."

"I'll listen to it."

"Ye shouldn't go undressed in here." He patted the heavy flamer he wore in a shoulder harness. "Be a hitter waitin' for ye outside. Ye won't get ten steps."

"What makes you think I'm not dressed?"

"If ye got it, ye better show it."

"I think I better not."

The man stared at him, rubbing his chin. "If ye got a phaser," he whispered, "I can get ye a thousand credits for it. Disruptor, two thousand."

Bones nodded seriously. "But if I had a phaser, and if I were willing to sell it, and if I gave it to you . . . well, I wouldn't be dressed any more, would I?"

"Ne problem. I can get ye anything ye want, in ten minutes. I'm a dealer, licensed."

118

Bones considered it. It probably would be a good idea to carry a weapon, if only to avoid trouble. "Could I buy something even if I'm not selling?"

"Sure. I got flamers, arrestors, tangleguns—"

"How much for a tanglegun?" They weren't lethal.

"You don't want one. Not unless ye got something else." Bones raised an eyebrow and smiled. "Fifty credits, five tax."

"I'll take it." As he said it, he realized he should have haggled.

"Fine." The man flicked his right wrist and a businesslike dagger appeared in his hand. He set it in front of Bones. "Meanwhile, put this in your belt." He stood. "Back in ten."

Bones walked around the place, soaking in the low life. A circle of men were playing some sort of game involving three sticks, where large sums of money changed hands rapidly. Others were playing more familiar games with cards and dice. He looked for a poker game but couldn't find one.

A rather shopworn woman made a pass at him— or at least an offer to do business—and Bones turned her down too politely, so she followed him around like a simpering shadow for several minutes. A supposedly blind beggar sat in a corner playing the accordian and croaking out bawdy songs. The dirty rag that covered his eyes probably hid nothing more than the bloodshot evidence of the previous day's excesses, but Bones liked the music and gave him a credit.

He finished off the corn and went back to try the grape. He beat the bartender down to Cr6.50 by threatening to go to another place, and began to enjoy himself immensely.

A fist-fight started and most of the clientele ignored it. Bones watched with professional interest, wondering whether he'd have to render aid. But the men were too intoxicated to do much damage to one another. After a few contusions and abrasions, they helped each other off the floor and staggered to the bar, arm-in-arm.

The weapons dealer came back. "Here ye go." The tanglegun was a large black pistol that fired a pellet that unfolded into a man-sized sticky net. A beat-up metal holster was included in the deal. Bones counted out the money and strapped it on.

"Know how to use it?"

"Oh, yeah." As a matter of fact, he'd never used one before. If things got tight, though, he could be beamed up in a matter of seconds. He gave the man back his dagger.

"Ye want to stick aroun' this place?"

"Seems congenial."

"Well, there's another place nearby, with girls," he said casually. "Dancers . . . Orion slave girls, best in the—"

"Yeah, I know. I've seen them." Sudden rush of desire: physician, know thy hormones. "Rough place?"

"Nay. Not even as rough as this. Cos' about twice as much."

In for a penny, doctor, in for a pound. "How far?"

"Not a kilometer. If we walked together, wouldn't have no trouble."

"All right." He drank down the grape, which was a little sweet for his taste. Maybe they'd have Denebian brandy there. "Let's go."

The night air was warm and smelled of alien spores. By starlight, Bones could barely see the path they were following, down toward the town.

His eyes got used to the light and he could see a figure walking up the path toward them. "Be ready to

120

draw," the man whispered. Bones wrapped his hand around the pistol's grip, enjoying adrenaline.

A couple of meters away from them, the man made a swift grab for his armpit. Bones snapped the tanglegun out and pulled the trigger.

Nothing happened.

He heard a faint click behind him and knew a split-second before the knife struck his back that he'd been set up.

It knocked him to the ground and felt like an icicle buried in his back. Trying to ignore the pain, he breathed cautiously. No trouble; it had missed his lung. Just below the plexus brachialis. Blood spreading slowly, not pulsing. If they'd just leave him alone, he would live.

The stranger emptied his pockets while the weapons merchant felt along his waist.

"Here we go." He reached under the shirt and unsnapped McCoy's communicator.

"Hey," the other said. "Ain't ne dightin' phaser!"

There was a stretch of silence. "Merd! It's a Fed'ration communicator . . . cove mus' be from that ship." He threw it away; Bones concentrated on remembering where it had landed.

"Fry the bastid?"

"Nay . . . if he dies, they'll stay 'til they find us. We can hide out in the fields 'til the ship leaves."

Bones heard them running down the path. Slowly, now. He inched toward the communicator, elbows and knees. Every time he moved his arms, the blade grated against a rib.

After a very long time, he found it. He pried the antenna open and put his mouth directly on the microphone.

"McCoy . . . to *Enterprise*," he whispered. "Beam . . . me . . ."

121

He fell unconscious just as a swirl of light enveloped him. He spent three days in sick bay (the rest of his shore leave), and kept the dagger as a souvenir.

Sharon Follett was taken back to the abrupt end of her first love—ended because of lies her supposed best friend had told the boy, to steal him.

Andre Charvat relived a time when his immediate superior had twisted the wording of a report around, to give himself credit for six months of Charvat's research.

Rosaly Ybarra: her first long trip away from home. She'd left her luggage with a new-found friend and gone off to adjust a ticket. When she came back, friend and luggage were gone, and she was stranded with only pocket change in a strange city where she couldn't even speak the language.

James Atheling: an infantile, almost nonverbal memory. His parents had left him alone in the house, perhaps to go shopping. It was night, and the power failed.

Atheling finished telling his story. "The overall theme seems to be one of betrayal."

Charvat nodded. "Treachery. Denial of trust."

"First it wanted to know about decisions," Bones mused. "Then betrayal. See a pattern, Spock?"

"One thing is obvious," he said. "After the last set of responses, the Arivne confirmed that it had used our memories in order to gather data about a process that was alien to it: decision-making. The phenomenon of betrayal—and by extension, trust—must be similarly alien.

"Perhaps it wonders to what extent it can trust us. Or, by a closer analogy to the first time—"

"*The analogy is correct.*" Hixon was still lying

down, but facing them. *"It is not humans we wonder about; you are powerless to harm us. We had to learn about betrayal so as to evaluate the Irapina proposal."*

"What did you conclude?" Spock asked.

The Arivne appeared; the "voice" changed. *"We have still more data to gather. Spock, you are physically the strongest . . . would you agree to an experiment that may cost your life?"*

"Explain it to me."

"We cannot. It might invalidate the result. The survival of your friends may depend on it."

"And my own, of course. I—"

"No. Only the pure humans."

Spock was silent for a moment, perhaps remembering two pure-human children. "Go ahead."

"Dr. McCoy, administer the drug."

"Not necessary," Spock said. "I am familiar enough with the state to induce it in myself spontaneously." He sat down and his eyes closed.

A slab of metal, two meters square by several centimeters thick, appeared on the ground in front of him, shiny purple-black. Spock rose, trance-like, and picked it up with one hand.

He put both hands close together on an edge, then pushed with one and pulled with the other. The metal bent slightly, with a deafening high-pitched creak. Where it was bending, it glowed red-hot . . . then orange, then yellow, then white—the blinding white of a star's surface. The others had to look away, and shield their faces from the heat.

With an awful rending sound, the slab gave way; Spock ripped it all the way through and dropped the two pieces. They fell heavily to the ground and imbedded themselves to a depth of several centimeters.

"That will do."

Spock came out of the trance and looked at the

two slabs, still glowing orange-hot along the tear. "Tritanium," he said. "I did that?"

"That is correct."

"But that isn't possible. Even if I could exert such a force, my bones and flesh lack structural strength to—"

"You did not do it alone. Many Arivne focused on you."

"What was the point of that?" McCoy asked. "Why did our lives depend on it?"

"They did not depend on it," the Arivne said. *"We are learning how to lie."*

With that, both the Arivne and Hixon disappeared.

"Very odd," Spock said.

"I'm getting used to it," McCoy said. "Now you see them, now you don't."

"Not that. These." He started to touch one of the slabs but felt the heat radiating from it, and withdrew. "Tritanium is 21.4 times as hard as the best steel.

"The illusion I experienced was of tearing a sheet of flimsy paper."

16

Mohammed Tafari sat back in the command chair and rubbed his chin reflectively. "Lissajous pattern? That's a globular search sweep, isn't it?"

"Yes, Captain," the navigator said. "Not an evasive maneuver at all."

He nodded. "Well, it just proves how deeply-seated their delusion is. They were searching for that mythical 'Anomaly' planet. Find their missing people . . . poor—"

Two strange creatures appeared on the bridge, in front of Tafari. One facing him; one with its back turned. Both had their hands raised, palms out.

"Not mythical, Captain. My planet. And I do hold their people captive."

Captain Tafari closed his mouth and stared for several seconds. His expression firmed. "Very impressive. I don't know how you do it, but it's very impressive." A phaser appeared in his hand. "Do you plan to capture some of us as well?"

"No. And you can put that away; it doesn't work."

Tafari elaborately put the phaser on "stun," aimed, and fired. Nothing happened. Then the phaser disappeared. "Also impressive. We're at your mercy, then."

"I am not interested in mercy; no more than I am interested in taking captives. We merely wish to be left alone. You will return to your legitimate mission."

He stiffened. "My mission is to capture the *Enterprise* and tow it back to—"

"Those orders were false. I gave them to you."

"That's absurd. I got them—"

"Easily verified."

He thumbed a button, not taking his eyes off Hixon. "Computer."

"Working," it said.

"Give me a summary of current mission status."

It paused, rather long. "Our current mission is to verify positions of bench marks in vicinity of Starbase 13, and search for reported debris from U.S.S. *Intrepid*. However, our position is wrong, and there are no data concerning our progress for the past 73 hours."

"Endit. Tabakow, get me Star Fleet Command."

"It will not work."

"He's right, sir."

"It, not 'he.'" He turned back to the aliens. "Just what do you think . . ." He was talking to empty space.

Kirk was startled, too. *"We have decided that you may come back. We have restored the coordinates to your computer."* And they were gone.

It was several seconds before anyone reacted. Kirk thumbed channel B. *"Enterprise to Lysander."*

The screen lit up with a picture of Tafari. He didn't say anything.

"Uh, Captain, Tafari, I don't know how to—"

"You too?" He shook his head. "We were told to resume our original course."

"And they've directed us back to Anomaly."

He kept shaking his head. "This is not," and he

sighed, "exactly what I signed up for. Do you have any idea . . . what those creatures are? Limitations they might have?"

"Not that I know of. One reason I've got to go back."

"And one reason I've got to go on—Kirk, it made my *phaser* disappear. It could make a piece of the hull disappear, too. For the safety of my . . ." Ironic scowl. "Myself and my crew, I must do as it . . . as it . . ."

"I understand."

He sat back. "Captain, I suppose we'll meet again. In court . . . as one another's witnesses."

"I suspect we will."

Hixon and the other hadn't been gone two minutes. They reappeared inside the stockade.

"What was that all about?" McCoy asked.

"We are bringing the Enterprise back. The situation now seems to require it. I will explain. But first, Mr. Spock, another test."

"I'm willing." He closed his eyes and sat down.

And suddenly, somehow, was sinking through the earth. Dirt, gravel, water table, glacial till—though there was no light, he could see everything—through the Mohorovicic discontinuity, into the mantle, where it was hot enough to melt rock, but the weight of dozens of kilometers of crust generated enough pressure to keep it from melting. As he moved, Spock felt the pressure as a caress; the temperature, summer sunshine.

What planet is this, he asked.

"It has no name."

Does it have life?

"None. Go ahead."

Feeling as well as seeing, Spock searched for a weak place. Found one: a crease in the discontinuity, a scar left under the ground from mountain-building. By some effort of will, that he didn't understand, he grew. Kilometers long and wide. He wedged himself into the crease; shoulders against one side, feet against the other. He pushed against the rock. Strained, joints popping. It shifted a hairsbreadth, complaining. He doubled his effort, clenching fists the size of houses. For some reason, this was important.

It gave way with a basso scream: pressure relieved, molten rock surged around him like warm water, hungry for the light of day, knocking him loose and bearing him toward the surface. He exploded out of a fissure and, sailing into the pale blue sky, surveyed his handiwork. It was too large to be called a volcano. It was a sudden traumatic incision through which the planet bled in great red spurts, molten rock spraying up and falling as deadly rain, falling on a surface that bucked and heaved as the rock beneath it subsided, seeking isostasy. Then the ocean marched in; a cliff of water from horizon to horizon, it swept to the fissure and didn't even have time to boil, but went directly from fluid to superheated steam, raving into the sky, tainted with the stink of sulfur; to Spock it was warm fragrant lover's breath—

Spock was sitting on the ground inside the stockade, his hands tightly clenched. He opened them and two pressed cylinders of dirt fell out.

"Remarkable." He dusted off his palms. "I was here all the time?"

"That's correct. Everything took place in your mind."

"I destroyed an imaginary planet. To what end?"

"A weapon. Your weapon against the Irapina.

"It is like this. The planet was only a complex symbol, a resistance for you to pit your will against.

128

It could have been any situation that was adequately challenging; it may be different next time.

"This is the way they fight.

"But they can only fight you this way through me. I have agreed to serve as a psychic go-between, so that they can evaluate your strength. What they don't realize, what I hope to keep from them, is that I am not just transmitting your will, but amplifying it. They are a practical race. If you seem too powerful, they will seek conquest elsewhere."

"You're doing this out of self-preservation, right?" McCoy said.

"Yes. It seems likely that the Irapina will betray us. They claim that we could coexist, after they defeat the Federation. But from what we've learned in experimenting with you, we think they are lying.

"Spock, if you had been fighting during this test, the Irapina would have been on the surface of the planet, either in his true form, or as a human or Vulcan. His will would have expressed itself as a geologic force, resisting your effort. If he won, you would be crushed. If you won, he would be immolated."

"Only in the illusion?" Spock asked.

"No. You or he would be dead, in reality."

"When is this duel going to take place?"

"Within hours. The Irapina say they are in the process of sending two 'champions,' actually scientists, who in fighting you will evaluate your performances.

"This is why I am bringing the Enterprise back ... Captain Kirk and you, Spock, seem to be the ones with the strongest wills.

"Remember, even if you fail in this, you will have forced the Irapina to squander energy, and will have given the Federation a full century's grace.

"When Kirk arrives, inform him as to what he

*will be expected to do. I will rest now, and return to
test him."* The Arivne disappeared.

Kirk materialized shortly thereafter, looking be-
wildered. The *Enterprise* was still several hours away.
Spock and the others filled him in.

"I wonder," Kirk said, "just how well they've
learned to lie. First the Irapina were coming here to
test them. Now they're coming here to test us. With the
Arivne in the middle . . . sounds fishy."

"Hixon!" Bones said. "What do you say about
that?" Hixon was lying down with his face away from
them, and didn't stir.

"We don't have any objective proof," Kirk said,
"that the Irapina exist at all. Just the Arivne's testi-
mony. It could be another one of its illusions, another
test."

"—rather than being the reason for the tests,"
Spock said.

Charvat shook his head. "It seems unlikely. What
reason would it have to lie to us? We're totally at its
mercy."

"Well, it might be still experimenting; setting up
new initial conditions," Atheling said. "It's seen how
we react to clear physical danger. Maybe it invented the
Irapina to see how we react to a purely abstract one."

"It really makes no difference," Spock pointed
out. "When the Irapina appear, we won't have any—"

The Arivne was back. *"I can't rest while you are
talking about me. Clatter, clatter. What can I do to put
an end to this speculation? We have little more than
an hour."*

"Give us some objective proof that the Irapina are
what you say they are," Kirk said.

*"What sort of proof would that be? I can show
you what they look like; I can project an image of*

130

their armada over your heads. But I could do those things whether they existed or not."

"True," Spock said. "Then at least would you explain why you first said they were coming to evaluate you, and then—"

"All right. I misrepresented you to them. They believe you are more powerful than you are.

"After they test you, they will test me. By participating in your experiences, I may learn how best to deal with them.

"At first, they were only peripherally aware of you. I exaggerated your potential so that I could use you as a buffer."

"To save your own hide," Bones said.

"Not really; not immediately. Our contest will be on a more rarified plane, and my life will not be in danger. Not for a thousand years, at any rate.

"I do not see this as treachery. It is true that your lives are in danger. It is true that I could have sent you on to the ship and faced the Irapina alone. But what if I had? This way, the Federation has more than a millenium of warning."

"Not if they kill us all," Kirk said.

"Easily solved." Everybody but Kirk and Spock disappeared. "They are back aboard the Enterprise. Now let me get some rest." With that, the Arivne was gone.

"Also a good idea for us," Spock said.

"True." Kirk watched Spock close his eyes and lie down, sleep coming instantly.

Then he spent the next hour looking at the walls, the lattice ceiling, the ground . . . and sweating.

17

Kirk's reverie was broken by the sudden appearance of McCoy.

The doctor shook his head violently. "Worse than the goddamned transporter."

Kirk nodded and checked his watch. "Must be about time. I wonder what it wanted you here for."

"Probably wants me to give you the pills. If you dose yourself, you're practicing medicine without a license."

The Arivne appeared. *"No. The Irapina were not frank with me. They have arrived, and there are three of them."*

"Wonderful," McCoy said through clenched teeth.

"You have little to worry about. The third is an immature individual of the organ-donating caste. It is little more than human."

"That's comforting."

Spock was wide awake. "Why weren't two sufficient?"

"They will observe the contest with the young one, to orient themselves. You may do so as well, if you wish."

Kirk nodded. "Where are they?"

"They lack the ability to teleport over short distances. They appeared before me where I was resting,

beyond the tree line, and are walking here." The drawbridge slammed down over the moat. *"They are here."*

The three Irapina walked into the stockade, their four legs giving them a strange undulating gait. Two were as the Arivne had pictured them; the third, obviously the immature one, was smaller, and its thorax was white.

Their arms moved constantly, like an insect's antennae, in nervous irregular circles. They smelled like soured milk.

"Can we communicate with them?" Spock said.

"Not directly. Through me, you can communicate in a symbolic, metaphorical way. That is what will happen during the contest. Are you ready, Dr. McCoy?"

"I suppose." He found the bottle of pills and swallowed two.

"Good luck, Bones."

He looked at Kirk and his voice broke. "See you later, Jim."

It was a poker game. Seven men around a green felt table. Murmured conversation, air thick with smoke. Shaded lamp hanging about a meter over the action. Everybody dressed in the style of the late nineteenth century—the riverboat gambler romance that had always been dear to Bones.

It was toward the end of a round of five-card stud. Bones had folded early; there were only two players left in the game. Large pile of red and blue chips in the pot.

The two players got their last cards, face up. One was a swarthy man in red velvet, who puffed nervously on a stogy. The other was a pale man with white hair, an albino, wearing a white linen suit with a string tie.

His pink eyes stared at Bones. He was the Irapina.

"Think I've got you," the dark man said. His last card had been an ace, giving him a pair of aces showing. He counted the chips that were in the pot. "Two hundred and seventy dollars." He counted out two gold chips and seven blue ones, and tossed them into the middle. "Cost you two-seventy." Pot limit, then: you could bet anything up to the size of the pot. A cutthroat game.

"Here is your two-seventy." The albino's voice had a metallic creak, like the chirp of an insect. He counted out nine more chips, mostly gold. "And I'll raise you eight hundred and ten."

Everybody studied the pale one's cards. His last one had been a deuce, giving him 2-4-6-5.

His opponent laughed harshly. "You ain't gonna buy this one." He started counting chips. "Three threes been out already. No way in hell you got the last one under there." He put in $2,430, the maximum.

It took most of the Irapina's chips: $7,290. "Raise you forty-eight sixty." The other players gasped.

"Goddamn it. You ain't gonna buy it." He had two small stacks of gold chips left. "You take a bank draught?"

"No. Chips or cash."

"Now how the hell am I gonna—"

A man standing behind him put his hand on his shoulder. "How much you need, Moser?"

"About four grand."

"I'll take your draught." He dropped four crisp bills on the table. "He's bluffing."

Moser counted out the rest of it and slid it into the middle. "Call. See you beat three aces."

With a long fingernail the Irapina flipped over his hole card. It was a three, completing the straight. He raked in the pot while everybody jabbered. The dark man stood up and lurched away.

134

Bones stared at the hole card. It was a three, all right, but neither heart, diamond, spade, nor club. It was a three of eagles, colored green. Nobody else seemed to think that was unusual.

The cards were collected and handed to Bones. He riffled through them and couldn't find the three of green eagles, nor any other odd card.

Bones had a couple of thousand in chips. He checked his wallet and there were twelve thousand-dollar bills. So he and the Irapina were about evenly matched.

He shuffled the cards and passed them to his right, to be cut. "Same game." Being a purist, five-card stud was his favorite. If only he could trust the deck.

Everybody anted ten and he dealt; one down, one up. He'd given himself a pair of kings, back-to-back. The Irapina also had a king, showing. He smiled and tossed in a stack of chips. "First king bets seventy."

"Aw hell, come off it," somebody said, and threw his hand in disgustedly. Two others also folded. The rest put in their seventy.

Another round: Bones dealt himself a third king. But the Irapina had two kings showing. The top one was the king of green eagles.

"Hold it," Bones said. Have to get control of this situation. "There's no such thing as a king of green eagles."

"Sure there is," the man next to him said. "House rule." Universal murmur of assent.

"First pair of kings," the Irapina said, "bets $420." The maximum, again.

Bones put it in; everyone else folded. He dealt the Irapina a card. In the air, it was a seven of diamonds. When it landed it was the king of green eggs.

Bones stared at it, concentrating. It started to change back to the seven, but stayed.

135

"Gonna give yourself a card?" somebody said. The deck was getting heavy, and felt cold. He started to peel one off the top and realized the cards had turned to metal, keen as razor blades. Trying to distract me. Small nicks on his thumb and forefinger.

He took a card: four of clubs. Concentrating, he turned it into the king of oranges.

"Boy howdy," someone said. "This is one hell of a hand."

The Irapina bet the maximum again. Bones called. He dealt. His opponent got the king of skulls.

A Navy Colt revolver appeared at the Irapina's elbow. "Give yourself a card," it said.

"What happens if we both have five kings?" he asked.

"Only nine kings in the deck," the man to his right said.

He picked his card gingerly off the top of the deck. It was impossibly heavy. He turned it over: king of clubs.

Bones already had the king of clubs, showing.

"Cheating," the albino said scornfully. He wrapped his hand around the butt of the pistol.

McCoy's pistol was a derringer, stuck in his belt. He could never reach it in time. The card grew larger and heavier.

As the Irapina picked up the Colt, he spun the card at him, a razor-sharp discus. It caught him in the throat. The gun discharged into one of the other players. The Irapina's head, severed from the neck, toppled onto the table. Bloodless, it rolled to the middle of the table, facing Bones.

Table, people, everything began to fade. "You know," the head muttered, "you're one hell of a bad sport."

The smallest Irapina lay on its side, headless. The stump of its neck oozed something thick and grey. Its head had rolled up against the stockade wall.

Bones was pale, trembling. "Guess we win the first round," he said weakly. His thumb and forefinger were still bleeding.

"Yes, but it was an immature one. Prepare your-selves."

"Which one of us goes?" Kirk said.

"Both of you at the same time."

"Will we share the same illusion?"

"Perhaps. Perhaps not."

Kirk was in the middle of a tug-of-war, on the Academy playing field. His squad against Jerry Novoski's, tugging on a big hauser rope, each trying to drag the other team into a juicy mud puddle between them.

Jerry was a good friend of Kirk's; they had made squad leader together. But there was something wrong. His expression was ferocious—and his eyes were pink!

They pulled back and forth for several minutes, neither team gaining a decided advantage. Suddenly, the mud puddle dries up. It becomes warm, then hot, and finally is a glowing bed of coals. Kirk is dragged to within a meter of it; he can feel the hair on his arms curling, crisping from the heat. He digs in and backs up a step. Two steps. The rope is starting to smolder.

Both teams strain until the rope unravels in a shower of sparks.

Spock was also engaged in a game.

He and the Irapina—a Vulcan with pink eyes—stood balanced on a smooth log railing, some six meters off the ground. A fall would be painful, but not fatal.

They were each armed with a padded club about a meter long. The object of the game was to thrust and parry until you either knocked your opponent off the log, or caused him to over-reach and lose his balance. Spock had done it dozens of times.

His opponent was good. He thrust lightly, experimentally, trying to find an attack which Spock might be clumsy in parrying. Spock was doing the same to him. They seemed evenly matched.

Suddenly it is warm, very warm. Without taking his eyes off the Irapina, Spock notices that the ground underneath them has burst into flame. The loser will die.

Since they are evenly matched, there is one logical move. He allows the Irapina an obvious opening. When he thrusts, Spock reaches forward and grabs his wrist, pulling them both off balance.

As they fall, the fire disappears.

Kirk was inside a battle satellite, spinning in a tight orbit around a black hole. He instinctively understood the situation: the Irapina was in an identical satellite, the same orbit, on the other side of the black hole. They each had ten missiles, old-fashioned nukes.

The Irapina launches one. It appears as a green blip on a holo screen in front of Kirk. It can't be launched straight at him in this "steep" a gravitational field; instead, it orbits the black hole, along with the two satellites, in a complicated series of precessing ellipses—like the Lissajous search pattern Kirk was familiar with. But each orbit takes little more than a second. The trick is to figure out from which direction the missile will be coming, when its orbit intersects yours. Launch a counter-missile in that direction. It has to be done by instinct; seat of the pants. Another one launched.

Kirk launches two against the Irapina—red blips —and tries to get a feel for the way the green ones are moving. Waste one missile and you'll be a sitting duck at the end of it. One of his red ones goes out. He wipes sweat from over his lip and sends out two anti-missiles. They find their marks, but two more green ones are in orbit now. He launches two at the Irapina and his fingers hover over the launching keys, analyzing the defensive situation. He decides.

Finally they each have four missiles in orbit, chasing one another, with one held in abeyance.

One by one, the blips go out. Stalemate.

Spock stood on a sort of see-saw arrangement, marked off by squares. He was two squares from the end. Another Vulcan, pink-eyed, was two squares from the other end; the platform was horizontal.

"Irapina," a voice says from nowhere, "what is the square root of 179?"

"13.3791," it says.

"Correct. Advance one square." The Irapina takes a step forward, and Spock's end of the see-saw slowly falls about halfway to the ground (it is not a simple fulcrum, but a complicated system of gears and pistons).

If his end touches the ground, it will contact a thick copper cable. Spock will be electrocuted.

"Spock," it says, "what is the natural logarithm of seven?" A harder question.

Spock does a rapid mental calculation. "1.94591."

"Correct. Advance one square." Level again.

"Irapina—"

"I protest," Spock says. "Being asked first, he has the advantage. You must ask me the next question."

"Well done. Advance one square." He does, and the other side dips down.

"Irapina, what is the atomic weight of zirconium?"

Child's play. "91.22," it says, and advances to level the machine again. They are both two steps from the middle. Spock tries to walk forward without waiting for a question, but his feet won't move.

"Spock, three to the fifteenth power."

Not too difficult. "14,348,907." He steps forward. If this game is being generated in his mind, what is the point, he wonders.

Only a test of confidence. The Arivne's voice.

They wind up together on the middle square. The pink-eyed Vulcan's breath smells of sour milk.

The deck shuddered under Kirk's feet as the last enemy ball struck amidships. That was the last one; both he and the pirate galleon had exhausted their ammunition. He surveyed the damage through roiling smoke.

The *Enterprise*'s mainmast was down, struck a glancing blow by a lucky long-range shot. It hung over the port side, the main skysail ballooning in the water. A small fire on the poop deck was under control. The pirate ship had all her sails, but in general was in worse shape. She was taking water; riding low and listing slightly to starboard. She was about ten meters away and closing. Most of her crew were crouched along the port rail with boarding hooks. Fires raged on her fo'c'sle and main deck. She would go down soon. When her crew boarded the *Enterprise* they would be a fierce enemy, with no avenue of retreat.

Such men as had pistols were waiting along the starboard rail, their targets drawing closer. They taunted the pirates; the pirates cursed back. Look for one with pink eyes.

A shot rings out and one of Kirk's men falls dead,

a great wound in his chest. The others raise their pistols.

"No!" Kirk shouts. "Wait ... choose a target and fire in volley, when the first hook comes in." A few people answer with "Aye, Sir"; no one fires. Someone retrieves the dead man's pistol.

Kirk loosens the hanger in its scabbard, touches the cocked pistol jammed in his belt. Seven men dead now, many more coming. The cabin boy runs across the main deck, scattering sand over the slick of blood. Good boy.

Don't get carried away. There is only one real enemy, and no real allies. Look for pink eyes?

"Yes."

His first mate lies dying beside him, legs shattered by a chain shot. Kirk is glad it isn't Spock.

Kirk draws his hanger and transfers it to his left hand. He draws the pistol and waits for a target, eyes.

A grapple on a rope sails through the air and clatters onto the main deck, and slips back to make fast on the rail. "Cut that!" someone orders, and the cabin boy rushes up with a knife. A sharp report and a terrible sight: the boy staggers back with half his head blown away. Someone fires in retaliation.

"Courage, lads!" Kirk shouts. "Wait for the hooks. If they can't board, they'll be food for sharks."

A dull boom and the deck shifts; the galleon's tilted keel has rammed the *Enterprise* below the waterline. The *Enterprise* rolls to starboard and, obeying a shout, the pirates' hooks dip down and grasp the rail. Kirk's men fire a ragged volley, then busy themselves casting off hooks that no longer have pirates attached to them. The pirates shoot back sporadically, at nearly point-blank range now, killing five more.

All illusion; ignore the moaning belowdecks, the stink of death and powder. Pink eyes.

A good try but not enough; the pirates are swarming onto the main deck, jumping down from their port railing with cutlasses swinging.

A pirate stands at the base of the gangway leading to the bridge deck. Staring at Kirk with black eyes. He raises his pistol—illusion, steady—and fires. The ball passes through Kirk and sails away. Another illusion cuts the pirate down from behind.

Almost too late, Kirk sees the one swinging toward him on a rope, strung from the galleon's mizzenmast. Pink eyes, pistol raised. They fire simultaneously, to no effect. The Irapina pirate collides with Jim and they both go sprawling.

Kirk squirms free, throwing the pistol away, shifts the sword to his right hand, and swings down in a cut. The Irapina parries with his cutlass and almost opens Kirk's belly with the dagger he's suddenly got in his left hand. Misses by a centimeter.

Failure of imagination: if Kirk visualized it, he could have a dagger in his left hand, too. Instead, he grabs a belaying pin from a bracket under the rail. Will serve for parries.

Kirk has a slight advantage—his hanger has a blade several centimeters longer than the pirate's cutlass—and he presses it. With rapid cuts and thrusts he forces the Irapina backwards, down the gangway to the main deck. But he can't lay steel on him; the alien's too fast. Try to wear him down.

Quietly in his ear: *"Remember, this is a contest of will, not skill. Whatever skill you have, he will automatically match. You must want more profoundly to live than he does."*

Through the melee on the main deck. Slice, lunge; never touching. Kirk tries not to notice as they work their way along the deck, that it's strewn with arms, heads: all illusion. The Irapina backs through a standing sailor as if he were a holographic projection, insubstantial. Kirk fights his way through the same man.

Is my progress a sign that my will is stronger? No answer.

He works the Irapina back to the gangway that leads to the poop deck. Up the steps, one by one. Get him up on the poop deck, Kirk thinks, and he can't keep backing away. Nothing there but Mother Ocean.

Going up the steps, Kirk notices that he has two shadows. Odd. That means there must be a double star behind him. He thought he was on Earth.

"Trickery, beware."

The starboard side of the poop deck is still smoldering from the fire. Force him over there.

The poop deck is deserted; Kirk has a feeling that all the other people have disappeared. No longer necessary for the illusion.

Spock was put inside a star, for a contest similar to his "planet-wrecking" exercise. He had a limited time in which to cause the star to explode, go nova. The Irapina would be resisting his efforts.

He had about ten minutes. Then he would slowly lose his invulnerability to the awesome heat and pressure inside the star, and would be destroyed. There would be no stalemate in this situation.

Fortunately, it was a double star. All natural novae start as double stars.

Still wondering about the double shadow, Kirk maneuvers the pirate toward the smoldering part of the deck. No flames, but here and there the oak decking glows dull red.

143

The pirate steps on a hot spot and jerks his boot away. Then his image shimmers, glows, and changes: it takes on its true form, insectoid centaur.

It no longer has cutlass and dagger, but parries well with its two chitin-hard arms.

Is this fair, Kirk wonders. The Irapina seems to have great resistance to heat; it's standing directly on the glowing coals.

"Kirk, Spock; beware. The two Irapina are collaborating."

Off the stern of the *Enterprise,* the other Irapina floats in a launch. Incongruously, it also has its true form.

Spock's star is a red giant, with a close red giant companion. He sees a way to make it explode.

The massive companion causes tides on the surface of his star, similar to Earth's lunar tides. The star, though, being elastic, is pulled out of shape. A huge spinning egg.

The gas that makes up the star is very turbulent —not only on the small scale of boiling and bubbling, but on a large scale as well: great masses of gas moving nervously around inside the star. This gives Spock a way to make it explode.

He knows that some very hot stars exist on the verge of being blown apart because of radiation pressure. The nuclear furnace in the core of the star blasts out so much radiation that it threatens to blow away the star's outer layers.

His star is too cool for radiation pressure to be much of a factor in its stability. The core of it, where he now floats, is preternaturally hot—it has to be, for atomic fusion to go on—but the atmosphere above it is too deep, too massive, for the radiation pressure to push away.

So his plan of action is to take advantage of the star's natural turbulence. Travel up toward the star's surface in a straight line, deflecting the masses of gas as they approach him. Riding a beam of hard radiation. Eventually the radiation pressure will be greater than the weight of the atmosphere above him. It will blow a planet-sized hole in the surface of the star (for Spock is himself planet-sized, here), which will upset the system's equilibrium. The star will go nova.

He starts swimming up. Naturally, he goes at a right angle to the direction of the star's companion (this is the shortest distance to the surface). It's hard work, since down this deep the star's gases are compressed so much that they are denser than metal. But he thinks he'll succeed, with time to spare.

"Kirk, Spock; beware. The two Irapina are collaborating."

What are they doing? Push. Push.

"They are both with Kirk."

Kirk is bathed in sweat. The Irapina doesn't attack; seems content to stand there and parry. Why is his back hot? The sun—*suns*—didn't seem that hot, earlier.

"All three are on a planet orbiting the star you are working on."

Then all three will be killed when it novas? Push, swim.

"They won't let it nova. Once the explosion begins, they will work together to restore equilibrium, and will probably succeed. You will have to start over."

But the initial explosion—

"That will be enough to kill Kirk. They are less affected by heat."

This is all illusion, Kirk thinks. But as Bones proved, it's illusion that can kill, as surely as a blade or a phaser (arivne: energy=matter=thought); can't slow down. But O God, it's hot.

The Irapina continues its waiting game.

Wonder how Spock's doing.

Push, swim . . . pause. So if I succeed, Kirk dies.

"That is correct."

Remembering *pon farr*. You've killed him once before, Spock. So either way, there will be one of us against two of them?

"Correct."

Spock juggles logic, morality, and a vestige of an emotion he might deny: love.

It will be Kirk. He stops swimming, and sinks back into the nuclear furnace.

18

From McCoy's point of view, the conflict was very subtle. Kirk and Spock sat on the ground, eyes glazed, twitching slightly. The two Irapina, likewise, stood almost motionless.

Then, evidently, it was all over. Kirk staggered to his feet, followed by Spock. The Irapina began moving their arms in circles.

Kirk: "What happened? Where's the ship?"

"The Irapina declared the contest invalid. Spock broke the rules. He stopped striving—but in triumph, not in defeat.

"He gave his life for yours. This is not allowed."

"Spock?" The Vulcan averted his eyes and nodded.

The Irapina began undulating toward them.

"Beware! They propose to decide the contest here. On a level of purely physical violence."

Kirk shook his head, trying to clear it. He was still in a drug fog. One Irapina charged him. Groggily, he raised an arm to ward it off. It grabbed his arm and threw him across the stockade.

Kirk slammed to the ground and fetched up against the log wall. He pawed at his belt but the phaser, of course, wasn't there. Nor the communicator. They bothered the Arivne.

Who spoke. *"Fool! Surrender to the drug! Let me take over."*

His left arm felt broken. His cheek was in the dirt and he couldn't summon up the energy to raise his head. The Irapina was advancing on him, looking impossibly large from ground level.

"Hear me! Surrender!"

Kirk couldn't figure out what the Arivne was talking about; he hadn't seen the tritanium-tearing demonstration with Spock.

But his body gave out. Even with the monster thundering down on him, he closed his eyes.

And had a short dream. He was sitting at a table. An ant walked toward him. For some reason it bothered him. He picked up a matchstick and used it to flick the ant away.

What Bones saw was Kirk calmly standing, tearing the stockade fence apart with his bare hands, holding the biggest log like a baseball bat, and swinging at the Irapina. Knocking it unconscious.

Spock did the same thing on the other side of the stockade. Bones had to do some fancy footwork to avoid the chunks of roof, as the structure collapsed.

The Irapina lay still on the ground, covered with rubble. After a few seconds, they faded away.

"We have succeeded," the Arivne said. *"The Irapina were also unsuccessful with the Organians."*

"They didn't realize you were amplifying our strength?" Spock asked.

"No. I made them think that I stood in a servile relationship to you, and to them as well. They couldn't understand a translator in any other terms. So they had nothing but contempt for me."

Kirk sat on a log, ghostly pale, his right arm cradling the broken left one. His eyes were red slits. "What happens now?"

"The Irapina will change course slowly over the next few centuries. They will go through the Orion Arm and eventually invade the Romulan Empire. I assume they will test the Romulans as they did us."

"I'm sure they'll get along well together," Kirk said. "Bones, do you have a pill?"

"Close your eyes." He did, and the left arm straightened out in front of him, healed.

"I could get you a job," Bones muttered.

"The Enterprise approaches orbit. I will send you there. When you leave, I will again erase any record you have of my planet's position. I ask that you not try to deduce it. Our races will not be able to meet again, to mutual benefit, for a long time."

"I'm sorry you feel that way," Kirk said.

"Please. Clatter, clatter." And everything turned to a shower of sparks.

Captain's Log, Stardate 6142.4:

Fortunately, the Lysander's subspace radio resumed working as soon as ours did, so they could partially corroborate our story. At least they won't be waiting for us with straitjackets.

Scientists on Starbase 4 may be able to detect the Irapina fleet, as far away as it is, because of the great mass of their vehicles. I confess I will be relieved if our experience can be confirmed by an outside agency, one too far away to be influenced by the Arivne.

He finished the log transcription and stood up. "Mr. Sulu?"

"Right away, sir." Five minutes early; that was unusual. He zeroed his console and locked it. Took the bridge.

Kirk nodded to Spock and they walked to the turbolift. Bones had asked them down for a drink before mess.

McCoy had broken out his last hoarded bottle of Denebian brandy; he could stock up again at Academy. He offered a toast:

"Well, here's to poor old Hixon."

They drank. Spock wasn't affected by the alcohol, of course, but he found the flavor interesting. "I don't think that we should pity him," Spock said. "If my own experience is any indicator, he's living more intensely, more confidently, than any of us ever will ... again."

Kirk nodded slowly.

"I learned something," Spock continued, "about myself. About power. Power over the physical universe and ... power over people." He glanced at Kirk. "It's difficult to put into words. Difficult even in Vulcan." He had tried to write it down the night before.

Kirk knew what he was talking about, though he hadn't attempted to record it; in fact, had tried not to think about it.

On the bridge deck of the good ship *Enterprise,* in the smoke swirl and battle clamor, salt air mingling with the stench of death, men standing fast and obeying him even to their certain death—he had learned something ruthless about himself. Why he lived for the joy of command. Why anger or fear could make his blood sing, and pull the corners of his mouth into a smile.

"I suppose you're right," Bones said. "I got something of that, in my poker game.

"In fact ..." he looked embarrassed; looked at his feet. "Last night I tried to recapture it. Put myself under hypnosis and made a recording."

"How did it come out?" Kirk asked.

"Nothing much. I can remember more of it while

150

I'm conscious. It's a pity, a damned shame. If we could get an objective record, personal fantasy so realistically amplified . . . it would be invaluable data for human psychologists. Vulcan, too."

"True enough," Spock said. He stared at the brandy's sparkling surface and remembered the glory of swimming through a star, and the different glory of surrendering to it. "But a lack of data is not the same as no information."

ABOUT THE AUTHOR

JOE HALDEMAN is a science fiction writer with degrees in astronomy and English. His novel, *The Forever War*, won the Hugo and Nebula Awards for "Best Novel of 1975."

Space . . . the final frontier.
These are the voyages of the Starship *Enterprise*

STAR TREK®

Relive the original five-year voyage of the U.S.S. *Enterprise* with Captain Kirk, Mr. Spock, Dr. McCoy and the rest of the crew in novels by such well-known science fiction authors as Joe Haldeman, David Gerrold, and James Blish. Bantam Books is proud to republish these all-original adventures (featuring stunning new cover paintings) based on what is arguably the most popular television series of all time.

☐ **PLANET OF JUDGEMENT** by Joe Haldeman (24168-0 • $2.50)

On a planet that cannot exist, Kirk and Spock fight for the very future of the Federation.

☐ **THE GALACTIC WHIRLPOOL** by David Gerrold (24170-2 • $2.75)

A beautiful young woman holds the key to Lieutenant Kevin Reilly's career—and the fate of her civilization.

☐ **WORLD WITHOUT END** by Joe Haldeman (24174-5 • $2.50 • Available July 15, 1984)

Captain Kirk and the crew of the *Enterprise* are held hostage inside an asteroid where technology truly is indistinguishable from magic.

Available wherever Bantam Books are sold, or use this handy coupon for ordering:

"A GREAT SPACE ADVENTURE IN A RICHLY IMAGINED FUTURE WORLD."
—Jack Williamson

THE ALIEN DEBT

by F. M. Busby
author of STAR REBEL and RISSA KERGUELEN

Here is a towering novel of challenge, survival and discovery by one of the modern masters of the science fiction epic. It is the stunning tale of humanity and their alien allies pitted in a clash against an alien race with horrifying telepathic powers. And at the heart of it all are Bran Tregare and Rissa Kerguelen—two bold, rebellious souls fueled by an indomitable spirit and fired by the courage to overcome immesurable odds.

"Busby writes fine adventure stories, the kind that made us love science fiction in the first place."

—Jerry Pournelle